MIDSUMMER
MADNESS

ASIS

MIDSUMMER MADNESS

Translated from the Spanish of
Emilia Pardo Bazán

By

AMPARO LORING

Fredonia Books
Amsterdam, The Netherlands

Midsummer Madness

by
Emilia Pardo Bazan

ISBN: 1-4101-0620-9

Reprinted from the 1907 edition

Fredonia Books
Amsterdam, The Netherlands
http://www.fredoniabooks.com

TO THE

MARQUIS OF CASA-LORING

IN REMEMBRANCE OF

KINDNESS SHOWN US IN MALAGA

FOREWORD

Doña Emilia Pardo Bazán, who wrote the original romance of "Midsummer Madness" in Spanish, is the most distinguished and best known woman novelist and critic in Spain today. She was born at Coruña in 1852, the daughter of the Count and Countess of Pardo Bazán, and belongs on both sides of her family to the oldest of the Galician nobility. At the age of sixteen she married Don José Quiroga, a country gentleman of Galicia, the "Switzerland of Spain," from which province her father was a deputy to the Cortes. The next few years of her life she spent in travel and study, specializing in German philosophy, and mastering the French, English and Italian languages in order to read the literature of those countries. She occupied a brilliant position at the court of Amadeo, and after the abdication of that monarch, shared the political exile of her father in Paris.

The first published work of Señora Pardo Bazán — for she has always written under her maiden name — was an exhaustive study of the life and works of Father Benito Feijóo, the Benedictine monk, famous in 18th century Spanish literature. In 1891 she was invited to lecture at the Athenaeum of Madrid, and these lectures were later published under the title, "The Revolution and Novel in Russia." She is credited by Spanish writers with introducing Russian literature to the Spanish public through these essays. The follow-ing year she lectured again at the Athenaeum on "The Franciscans and Columbus." Señora Pardo Bazán has not only written about fifteen successful novels, but her ambitious versatility has led her to seek dis-tinction and fame in literary criticism, verse, books of travel, lectures and polemics. Her book entitled "The Question of the Hour" made her leader of a new literary school in Spain. In this work she championed the cause of Realism as opposed to the Naturalism of Zola's school, although at the same time doing ample justice to the power and poetic beauty of much of Zola's work. Surface resemblances between her work and the French master's writings have led many, even of her own country-men, to class her as an adherent of the Naturalistic school. Leading critics claim that her "La Tribuna" is a Naturalistic tale in which the influence of Zola and his school is unmistakable. Her novel, "The Corner Stone," ("La Piedra Angular") called forth much discussion from French and Italian anthropologists. In 1892 Señora Pardo Bazán was invited to serve on the committee of the Pedagogical Congress held at Madrid, and that same year she edited a series of publications known as the "Women's Library," and translated many of the best works of French and Russian Realists.

She is an ardent upholder of the equal rights of men and women in all educational, social and political matters, one of her cleverest essays being a discussion of John Stuart Mills' theories concerning the political position of women. Perhaps her greatest "tour de-force" was the publication for three years of a peri-odical called the "New Theatre of Criticism." a title borrowed from the work of her celebrated fellow Galician, Benito Feijóo. Everything that appeared in the "Theatre" was from her pen, and each number contained a short story besides excellent essays on topics of the day, research subjects, reviews of books, etc.

The novels of Doña Emilia Pardo Bazán have been translated into French, and some of them into Russian, Swedish and English. Her works are the most frequently quoted, applauded and decried of any in contemporary Spanish literature. An American critic compares her Realism in depiciting action to that of our own William Dean Howells, while the Portugese critic, Pinnheiro Chagas, calls her the most remarkable woman author in Europe since George Sand.

AMPARO LORING.

Boston, Massachusetts,
   November, 1906.

MIDSUMMER MADNESS

CHAPTER I

THE first sign which told Asis Taboado that she had emerged from the limbo of dreams was a sensation of pain, as though her temples were being bored through and through with a fine gimlet. Then the roots of her hair seemed to turn into a million needlepoints, pricking through to the brain. Her mouth felt bitter, her tongue dry, her cheeks burned and her veins throbbed. Her whole body was declaring in its dumb way that although the rising hour had come, it was in no condition to make any exertion.

She sighed, and in turning over discovered that every bone ached. She grasped the bell-cord, and rang sharply. The maid tiptoed in, and began to open the dressing-room blinds. A ray of sun shot into the chamber, but Asis called out in a hoarse, weak voice,

"Not so wide — leave them only a crack open — like that."

"Is Madam feeling better?" asked Angela, solicitously — she was familiarly known by the nickname of Diabla.

"Yes, but my head is splitting still. You may make me a cup of tisane."

"Very strong, Madam?"

"Not very."

Diabla said she would bring the drink in a minute, which presently lengthened into fifteen. Meanwhile her mistress turned to the wall, and drew the sheet up over her face to comfort her burning cheeks with the cool linen. From time to time a stifled groan escaped her. Asis had never felt such a buzzing in her head except once when she had visited the Royal Mint, and rushed out half crazy from the stamping room. Surely the machinery of the Mint was now working within her skull! She felt as though a legion of demons were amusing themselves by pulling out her brains, and winding them off on red-hot reels! Moreover, she was conscious of an inward perturbation. The bed appeared to swing like a hammock, and with every movement a new qualm seized her.

At last came the tisane, skilfully brewed and steaming hot. Asis sat up with her hands pressed to her temples. At the first taste a sudden, real nausea attacked her.

"Why, this is boiling; I've burned my tongue," she groaned. "Support my shoulders, Angela. That's better."

Diabla was a wide-awake girl, a Luguesian able to give points to the keenest daughter of Andalusia.

She looked askance at her mistress, and asked with apparent concern,

"For heaven's sake! Is Madam feeling worse again? I believe this is what we call sun-fever at home, for yesterday was hot enough to melt paving-stones, and Madam was out the whole blessed day!"

"Yes, it must be that," sighed the lady.

"Does not Madam wish to send for the Doctor Sanchez del Abrojo?"

"Nonsense. I wouldn't trouble the doctor for a trifle like this. Pour the tisane into a glass."

Several pourings cooled the drink. Asis swallowed it, and turned again to the wall.

"I shall go to sleep," she said. "I do not want to eat, but let the servants take their breakfast now. If any one calls, say I am out. Be ready when I ring."

She spoke in the ungracious tone of one whose mind and body are alike overstrained.

When at last the maid had withdrawn Asis sighed still more deeply, and pulled up the sheets again, muffling herself in a shroud of linen. She arranged the folds of her nightdress to cover her feet, threw back her tangled mass of hair, moist with perspiration and harsh with dust, and then lay quite still, experiencing growing relief and physical comfort from the calming infusion.

The headache had beat a retreat as soon as the hot drink reached the stomach; the fever and nausea diminished. Yes, so far as the body was concerned she felt infinitely better, but the mind? What train of thought was coursing through her brain?

Beyond a doubt the waking hour is the time of the whole day when conscience enjoys completest empire. Colors are readily distinguished after the night's rest, with its parenthesis of sleep. Ambitions, desires, affections, hatreds — all are sunk in a kind of mist. The excitement of exterior life is absent. As after a long journey our starting point seems to have faded out of existence, so, on awakening, the cares and fevers of the previous day appear to have vanished in smoke, never to return for our torment. The bed is a curtained cell where we meditate and examine our consciences all the better because we are comfortable, and neither noise nor light distracts our thoughts. Our bitterest heartaches and our best resolutions often remain between the blankets.

Some perception of all this doubtless passed through our heroine's mind, but among and above all other thoughts ran a feeling of intense astonishment.

"Is this really true? Is this my story? Good God, am I dreaming awake?"

And although the Creator did not trouble Himself to answer, that force which resides in some part of our moral natures, and speaks to us with the authority of a divine voice, did reply.

"Arch-hypocrite," it said, "you know the truth but too well. Ask me no questions. My answers will make you writhe!"

"Diabla is right," thought Asis.   "Yesterday I had a touch of the sun, and it has gone to my brain.   This Madrid is a seething cauldron.   Delightful summer weather, indeed !   I am well paid for venturing into that hornet's nest !   At this time of year I should be home, in Galicia."

Doña Francisca Taboado felt a little easier when she had laid the blame on the sun.   No fear that the King of Stars would dart the least ray of protest. Although he is less accustomed than the moon to be called a go-between, we may suppose that he receives such accusations with equal impassibility.

But the inflexible voice made itself heard once more.

"Acknowledge, at all events," it insisted, "that if you had taken nothing more than a sun-bath — come, never attempt to impose on an old friend like me ! You and I have wintered and summered each other these two and thirty years.   Subterfuges count for nothing here.   No manner of use to plead that it was unexpected, or this, that and the other.   My blessed child, the pitcher goes often to the well.   There is no doubt about this matter.   Until now you have been irreproachable ; very good.   You have supported two years of mourning with dignity ; the more to your credit, I admit, because at the last it must have required some virtue to love your uncle, husband and natural lord, the noble Marquis of Andrade, with his dyed whiskers and his many ailments.   In spite of a

natural love of gaiety, no one has seen your shadow,
except in church and at the houses of your most intimate friends; well done! You have devoted long
hours to your daughter, like the affectionate mother
you are; no one denies it. You have determined to
bear yourself always as a lady, to enjoy your position
and independence, to indulge in no intrigues, to keep
your hands off forbidden fruit ; I recognize your pru-
dence. But, my dear, what of all this ? For one
single moment you lowered your guard; you committed an imprudence — and of the most dangerous
type. Along comes the Tempter; he casts his net.
Behold you in a moment grovelling on all fours among
the vulgar herd of sinners ! Don't talk to me of the
sun here, and the heat there. Bad excuses of an in-
solvent debtor. You have not even the common
plea of a caprice, a mastering passion. No, my girl!
a mortal sin, in cold blood, without extenuating circumstances. Well done!"

The grateful influence of the tisane lessened under
these irrefutable arguments. The terrible restless-
ness and suffocation began to return. The gimlet in
Asis's temples became a corkscrew, tugging to draw
her brains out, like the stopper from a bottle. The
bed burned, the culprit's body as well. She turned
and tossed like Saint Lawrence on his gridiron, seeking a cool place on the edge of the mattress. Convinced at last that every spot was equally hot, she
jumped up, and, like a white, still phantom in the

curtained room, glided to the basin, turned the faucet, and dipping her hands in the cool water wet her face, rinsed her mouth, and bathed her eyelids for a long time, with most happy results. This accomplished, her ideas became clearer, and the point of the cork-screw retired somewhat from her brain. Blessed relief! To bed, to bed again! Close, eyelids; stir not, muscles; silence and oblivion!

Oblivion is easily said, but how stop the thinking machinery? As throbbing, aching, burning quieted themselves, recollection became more piercing, the cavillings of conscience became more active and demoniac.

"If I could pray!" groaned Asis. "Nothing makes one so sleepy as to recite the same prayer mechanically over and over again."

And she tried to pray. But if the action proved soporific in one respect, in another it served to aggravate her moral inquietude, calling up the image of her spiritual director. What would Father Urdax say to this unheard of, stupendous confession? A confessor so stern about *décolleté*, absence from mass and other trifles incident to life at court! What periphrases might best soften his first impression of horror, turn the edge of his first lecture? Periphrases, indeed! With that blunt questioner, so regardless of one's reticence or shame! That powder-mill ready to explode at the least touch of flame! That rigid Jesuit of the old school!

But if he would allow one to explain things from the very beginning, with minuteness enough to show the fatality, the train of circumstances which — But who would dare make use of certain excuses with that determined, penetrating Jesuit ? The priesthood expect every one to be rabidly virtuous. They admit of no compromises, no palliations. People pretend that formerly the priests were too tolerant, but that is very doubtful ; and as for the present day —

In spite of a melancholy conviction that with Father Urdax it would be waste of time and breath to say anything except " I accuse myself of — " Asis composed in the dusk and silence of her chamber the following narration, in which it is clear that she refrained from showing herself in the worst light, and strove to emphasize the mitigating circumstances, of which, dear reader, there were surely few enough.

CHAPTER II

LET me go back a little to report what happened, or rather what was said day before yesterday, at the Duchess of Sahagun's reception. I am a regular attendant at those weekly gatherings, and so is my fellow Galician, Don Gabriel Pardo de la Lage. Don Gabriel is a major of artillery, a model gentleman, although somewhat *naïf*, very eccentric, and possessed by certain odd ideas which he advocates at times with the greatest warmth and persistency. But for the most part he remains in his shell, or devotes himself to *tresillo*, without concerning himself about what is going on in our circle. Nevertheless since I have become a regular Wednesday night guest it has been noticed that he is more apt to join the group of ladies ; and he seems to enjoy engaging the hostess and myself in argument. On this account certain persons say that Don Gabriel is not indifferent to my charms ; but others declare that he is hopelessly in love with a cousin or niece, and that she is the heroine of I don't know what extraordinary romance. Be that as it may, the Major and I, with all our disputes, are far from enemies. Enemies ! Each argument seems to increase our mutual sympathy, and I feel as though his moral peculiarities (I don't know what else

9

to call them) were beginning to appeal to me as the indication of a certain largeness of soul. That is very lamely expressed, but I have the idea clearly enough.

To come back to the subject. Day before yesterday the Major was evidently ripe for a discussion, and from the first moment he had us all convulsed with his bold paradoxes. He had hit on the commonplace that Spain is as uncivilized as Central Africa; that our veins are filled with African, Bedouin, Arabic and heaven knows what other wild blood; that all this paraphernalia of railroads, telegraph lines, factories, schools, learned societies, political freedom and daily papers is purely artificial — stuck on, as it were, with gum, and, in consequence, loosening and dropping off from time to time. He maintained that the only genuine, national part — our barbarism — holds its own, and promises to endure forever. Imagine the tempest drawn down on him by this declaration! My first retort was to compare him to the French, who set us down as fit for nothing but to dance the bolero and clink the castanets. I added that of course the educated classes are the same the world over.

"Now, look you, that is precisely what I deny at the start!" cried Pardo, with tremendous energy. "This side the Pyrenees every one, without exception, is a barbarian; the society people just as much as the street Arabs. The single difference is that we of the higher class dissimulate a little better — from shame, on account of social conventions, or for our own convenience.   But let the path incline ever so little before us, and we slide.   At the first ray of Spanish sun (that much abused sun, target of foreign criticism, which is seldom to be seen, since it rains here as much as in Paris) — "

"Go on, Pardo," I interrupted.   "Deny that we have a sun at all!"

"No, I don't deny the sun.   How could I?   Closely as we muffle up in winter to guard against pneumonia, in summer Madrid turns into a seething cauldron, in which we all stew together.   In truth, the summer no sooner makes its appearance than we are seized with a diabolical excitement, a veritable midsummer madness!   The sun goes to our heads, and all distinctions of class and education disappear before the general ferocity and vulgarity."

"Oh! I see what you are driving at; the bull-fights!"

For, really, Pardo is absolutely mad on that subject. It is one of his favorite and most frequent topics. You should hear him revile the amateurs of the sport, and tax the ring, as Father Urdax taxes the wicked Piñata balls, and plays like Demi-Monde.   How he thunders out about the three wild beasts, the bull, the bull-fighter and the public!   The first, which lets itself be killed because it can't help it; the second, which kills for money; the third, which pays to see butchery, and is consequently the most ferocious of all.   And then about the Pope's excommunication on those who attend bull-fights, and about the terrible loss to agriculture! On the last head Pardo makes some astonishing statements. If one were to credit him, the bull-fights are responsible for the deficit in the treasury, and for our two civil wars! But to be quite just, Don Gabriel made this last statement in a moment of great excitement, and half retracted when we took him to task in a body.

This is why I thought I saw the bull's horns sticking out behind "ferocity" and "barbarity"; but I was mistaken, for Pardo replied,

"Leave the bulls out of the question, though for that matter they illustrate the barbarizing influence of the sun well enough. Isn't it proverbial that without sun there is no good bull-fight? But leave them out of the question, I say; for I do not wish to seem a monomaniac on the subject of the horned gentry. Take any other genuine manifestation of our national life, something eminently Spanish. It is fair-time now. Isn't to-morrow the feast of Saint Isidro? Will not the people be taking their holiday on the hills and in the meadow?"

"Pardo, you are not going to criticise the fairs and their patron saints into the bargain? Isn't the Court of Heaven safe from your attacks?"

"Truly, the Saint is honored in his feast. An admirable Saturnalia his devotees offer him. If Saint Isidro, that gentle and honorable cultivator of the soil, could see the spectacle, he would turn the roasted beans into pebbles, and rain down fire from Heaven on his adorers. That festival is one of Pluto's pig-styes. There the most characteristic Spanish instincts run riot, and display all their native brilliancy. Orgies, quarrels, stabbing frays, gluttony, robbery, sacrilege and indecency of every description. A fine picture, ladies! That is the Spanish people, with the check-rein loosened. They are like colts let into pasture for the first time; all their delight is in running, neighing and kicking like mad."

"Oh!" I cried, "if you are talking of the lower classes only —"

"No; I insist upon it that we are all the same in virtue of our race. The instinct is alive at the bottom of our natures; place and occasion are the elements which determine whether we observe the restraints imposed on us by education — mere cloaks or husks at best."

"What theories, merciful heavens! And you admit no exceptions for our sex? Are we savages, too?"

"Certainly, and perhaps more savage than we men, for, after all, your education is more limited than ours, and — worse. Don't be offended, friend Asis. I will concede that you are as little a savage as possible, for certainly our native Galicia is the most peaceable and reasonable province in Spain."

At this point the Duchess turned round in surprise. During our discussion she had been conversing with a stranger, a good-looking young Andalusian, son of a rich land owner of Cadiz, who was an old friend of the Duke's. The Duchess admits none but intimate friends to her receptions, and it is only by an accident such as this that one ever sees a strange face at her house. But distant as she is with new acquaintances, the Duchess jealously cherishes all old intimacies, and treats us with such constant affection that we one and all praise her as the model of faithful friendship. This virtue, by the way, flourishes more freely at court than is generally supposed. I had noticed that while devoting herself to the stranger's entertainment the Duchess was lending one ear to our conversation, and seemed anxious to take sides in the dispute. Here was an opportunity to join us, and introduce the stranger gracefully. She seized it with delight.

"Many thanks, Don Gabriel, in the name of all Andalusians! You Galicians are forever tearing us to pieces, and now you are coolly classing us with the savages!"

"Oh! Duchess, Duchess!" replied Pardo, with great suavity, "could you imagine for a moment that I referred to you? An intellectual woman, a patroness of the fine arts! An amateur of Moorish jars and Assyrian jugs! The owner of a mineral-cabinet which makes the German Embassador green with envy! You, Madam, who actually know the meaning of the word fossil! You, the terror of certain would-be erudites of our acquaintance!"

" No flattery, Pardo. To hear you, any one would think me a blue-stocking! Surely one may admire a bit of porcelain or a picture. But don't imagine, my friend, that you can divert us so easily from the question of barbarism. What do you think, Pacheco? According to our friend, a Galician himself, Spain is peopled with barbarians, and Andalusia most of all! Asis, let me present Don Diego Pacheco. Pacheco, the Marchioness of Andrade — Don Gabriel Pardo."

Without saying a word the young man rose and took my hand, at the same time bowing low. I murmured between my teeth the phrases we always murmur in such cases. This ceremony over, we looked at each other with the cold curiosity of first acquaintance, when lack of interest prevents observation of details. Pacheco wore his evening dress with an air of distinction. Had I not known him to be an Andalusian I should have thought him English from his complexion and features. I set him down as a serious fellow, little given to chattering and arguing.

In reply to the Duchess's question he said in the lazy Southern drawl,

" Of course every one thinks his own country best. Andalusia has done nothing to merit the title of savage, for we have our poets, painters, authors and all that, while our lower classes are admitted to be particularly polite and intelligent. I must protest against what was said about the ladies. This gentleman will not deny that they are all angels."

"If we are talking gallantry," replied Pardo, "I will admit anything you like. But generalization proves nothing. In national units I see neither men nor women ; I see a race tending historically in this direction, or in that."

" Ah! Pardo," exclaimed the Duchess, in her most winning tone, "leave this splitting of hairs and these intricate philosophical arguments. Speak out in good plain Spanish, and remember that we who are not philosophers are in danger of losing your point through sheer ignorance."

"Very well, then, in plain Spanish I say that He and She are moulded of the same clay — there being but one kind ; so that here in Spain (here goes, since you ask me to speak out), the women also pay their tribute to barbarism. This fact may not be patent at first sight, because their sex obliges women to adopt smoother manners, and condemns them to the rôle of angel, as our new friend says. Take our friend Asis, a native of northeast Spain, where the women are quiet, gentle and affectionate. Nevertheless let her feel the influence of the sun, and I wager she would be capable of the same atrocities which the daughters of the people commit."

" Oh! my friend," cried I, "you are incurable. The sun must bear the burden now. What has the poor orb done to you, that you abuse him so ? "

" It may be an idle fancy," said Pardo, "but I believe we carry his influence like wine in our veins.

When we least expect it the subtle spirit goes to our brain, and takes our reason prisoner."

"That fancy, at least, cannot apply to Galicia, for there the sun hides his face so many days of the year."

"Well, then, never mind the sun. Say it is the Spanish air. I will admit that, after all, the Galicians differ from the inhabitants of the rest of the peninsula in appearance only. Have you observed how kindly we are taking to bull-fights ? In Marineda the Square is always crowded, and the throng gets as much excited as they do in Seville or in Cordova. The cafés where the national songs are sung have become the rage. The men go wild over the café singers. Hundreds of knives are sold, and used, too, more's the pity. The very street boys have the bull-fighter's slang at their tongues' end. Manzanilla runs in rivers in the Marineda taverns ; demijohns, black-jacks, everywhere. An absurd parody on the real thing, I grant you, but a parody which would be impossible were not the good people eager to run themselves into the mould. Take my word for it, since the Restoration we Spaniards have done nothing but encourage each other in absurdities. The farce began with the demonstrations against Don Amadeo — that nonsense of mantillas, high combs and short flounced skirts. Then came the late king's mania for the national type, imitated, as was to be expected, by the whole body of good society. To-day the simple fad has developed into an epidemic, so that between bull-fights, guitar-scraping, *jotas*, red and yellow tasselled tambourines, and fans adorned with the portraits and deeds of Franscuelo and Mazzantini we have constructed a comic-opera Spainkin, like one of Goya's pictures, or a burlesque by Ramon de la Cruz. Protests are of no avail; it is the fashion, and we must follow it. Look at our dear Duchess, a model of culture, courtesy and all womanly qualities; wouldn't she feel delighted to be called the wittiest wench in Madrid?"

"Indeed I should, if it were true," cried the Duchess, with her customary vivacity. "One Spanish 'wench,' to use your own words, is worth thirty foreign sticks. I detest the fashion of imitating foreign customs, for I am Spanish through and through, do you understand? It is far better to appear as God made us than to strain after the fashions of other countries. Look at the craze for living like the French or the English; what could be more absurd? France sends us our finery, and that is well enough, for no one wants to be a fright in the fashions of eighteen hundred and frozen to death. England has taught us to roast meat, and that is about all. But tell me, my worthy friend, how do you make out that Spain has remained barbarous, while the rest of the world has become civilized? In the first place, may one know just what you mean by barbarous? And in the second place, what does our poor, unfortunate country do more than the rest of Europe? Answer me that!"

"Ah! Duchess, you overpower me — I scarcely know what I am saying. Heaven help me, then! I will return to my first example. Have you ever visited the Fair of Saint Isidro?"

"Of course I have, and it is the most interesting and picturesque sight. What rich types! Those swings! Those dare-devil fellows everywhere, the indescribable animation in the human swarm! I just love the sight of popular festivals of this class. Suppose there are roughs and drunkards by the score; wouldn't you find the same in staid Holland? Do you imagine that in Merry England people never fight, never swear, and never take a drop too much?"

"Madam," cried Pardo, in a tone of discouragement, "you are an enigma to me. Such refinement of taste in some directions, such indulgence for the brutal and ferocious in others! I can explain it only by considering that while you are gifted with heart and head of superior calibre, you belong to a Byzantine, a decadent generation, which has lost its ideals. I will say no more now, or you will be laughing at me and my theories."

"That is a very seasonable fear, if it keeps you from using philosophical terms which I do not understand," replied the Duchess, with her low, silvery laugh. "Don't mind this man, Marchioness," she continued, turning to me. "If you listen to him you will become a Quaker. Instead of that, take my advice. Go to the Saint Isidro to-morrow, and see for yourself who is right. Our Don Gabriel has discovered that the Spaniards are the only people on the face of the earth who drink too much! As for the English, they never get tipsy, and beat their wives!"

"Dear Madam," returned the Major, rather red, but still smiling, "the English certainly do intoxicate themselves shamefully, but it is with sherry or beer, or some of their infernal alcoholic drinks; never in our fashion, with the air, the water, the bustle, the music and the light of heaven. After drinking they are like monkeys, but we are like ferocious beasts. We are possessed by the wicked spirit of boasting and bullying; we run into the worst follies in pure sport, taking pains to imitate the lower classes, men and women alike, let but the occasion present itself. Duchess, let us compromise with everything except vulgarity."

"No one can say," replied the Duchess, "that the Marchioness and I have furnished any cord for scandal to twang on."

"Every cat provides some fiddle at last," said Pardo, sententiously.

"Let us continue the figure and scratch the slanderer's eyes out!" cried the Duchess, in mock fury.

"Why don't you come to our assistance, Pacheco?" said I, turning to my silent neighbor. I found that he was looking steadily at me. Without moving his eyes, he excused his neutrality by declaring that we were defending ourselves so successfully as to be independent of any aid. A few minutes later he looked at his watch, took leave laconically, and retired.

His departure completely changed the conversation. Of course, we began to discuss him. Our hostess explained that she had invited him as the son of a valued friend. "But," she added, "although he looks as indolent as a Moor, and as reserved as an Englishman, he is really an accomplished rake. Good form, a gentleman, of course, but a Don Juan Tenorio for audacity and success. His poor father has been unable to curb his extravagance or shame him out of idleness, for he will set himself to nothing but turning women's heads." Here the Major, who is like others of his sex in disliking to hear that another man is a favorite with women, shook his head, and muttered low, as if to himself,

"A good sample of our modern Spanish race!"

CHAPTER III

THE next morning was the feast of the Patron of Madrid, so I started out early to hear mass at Saint Pasqual's. Heaven knows that as I walked along in my mantilla, prayer-book in hand, I had no thought of anything romantic. Indeed, had any one ventured to predict what was about to occur, I should have had him arrested on the spot for libel. As it was a little early, I walked down Alcala Street, and I remember passing the Suizo, and hearing some absurd compliments from the men in tight trousers and short jackets, whom one always sees lounging about that spot. "What great black eyes you have, my beauty! Long life to the priest who baptized you in extra dry sherry!" and more in that vein. I could scarcely keep my countenance on hearing their ridiculous expressions; but I made a dignified effort, and quickened my pace to get away from the group.

Passing the open space about the Cybele Fountain, I began to notice the remarkable beauty of the day. Never was air purer or sky clearer. The acacias in the Recoletas exhaled a heavenly perfume, and the trees looked as fresh as if they had donned a new suit of green in honor of the Saint. I felt so young that I could hardly resist the temptation of running and skipping along the green walks. I doubt if ever, even as a child, did I experience so strong a sense of vitality, such a desire to do something extravagant; to tear off the branches, for instance, or dive into the basin presided over by the good lady with the lions. Nothing short of the commission of such childish follies would have expressed my body's gladness.

I continued down towards Saint Pasqual's, but my mind was distracted, my religious fervor half evaporated. A few steps from the church I noticed a man leaning against a great sycamore tree. At sight of me he tossed away his new-lighted cigar, and came forward, hat in hand. In another minute a pleasant Andalusian voice was saying,

"Good morning, Marchioness. What happy chance brings you here alone, so early in the day?"

"Oh! Pacheco, is it you? And what brings you here, may I ask? I am sure you are not on your way to mass."

"How do you know that? Why shouldn't I be going to church, too?"

We exchanged these greetings while shaking hands. The familiar cordiality with which we both spoke was really astonishing, considering that we had met for the first time the previous night, and had not exchanged a dozen words in all. No doubt the magnetic air influenced us to communicate our physical satisfaction, and gave to our actions and voices an especially expansive character. As I am speaking in

confidence to my conscience, and may hold back
nothing, let me frankly admit that the Andalusian's
attractive exterior may have accounted for some part
of my cordiality.   Indeed, why is a woman debarred
from thinking a man handsome?   Why should it be
counted bad taste in her to show that she does think
so?   If we refrain from expressing such thoughts, be
sure they are in our minds; and what is more dangerous than hidden feelings which seethe within?
The truth is that Pacheco, in his well-cut suit of light
cloth, was as charming a gallant as one would see in
a summer day.   Still, his personal appearance did not
occupy me beyond a few seconds, for I do not regard
the outside alone.   Didn't I give good proof of that
in marrying my uncle, when I was twenty, and he
upwards of fifty, and far from well-preserved?

To resume.   Pacheco ignored the church bells,
which were just beginning to ring, and followed up
his opportunity by engaging me in lively chat.   We
soon took refuge under the plane-tree, for the sun dazzled us so that we could scarcely hold our eyes open.

"What an early bird you are this morning," he
began.

"Early, because I am out for ten o'clock mass?"

"Yes, indeed; any time before lunch is early."

"Well, you are as early as I, this morning."

"You see I had a presentiment of good luck —
The bull-fight will be fine this afternoon, they tell
me.   Are you going?"

"No; the Duchess of Sahagun will not be there, and I generally go with her."

"Are you going to the races, then?"

"No, indeed; the races bore me. It is nothing but a review of old nags, and I do not understand book-making. The only interesting part is the march."

"Well, then, why not go to the Fair?"

"To Saint Isidro? After Don Gabriel's sermon yesterday?"

"I know that you don't mind his talk."

"Would you believe it, in all the years I have lived in Madrid I have never seen the Hermitage, even!"

"Is it possible? You must see it, then; it will amuse you immensely. You remember the Duchess said last night that the Fair was well worth a visit. I have never been out there either, but, then, I am a stranger in Madrid, you know."

"And what of the brawls, the knife-thrusts, and all that Don Gabriel railed so against? Do you think that he was drawing on his imagination?"

"I don't know about that; but what does it matter?"

"You make me laugh when you say so coolly, what does it matter? Suppose I should get a bad fright in the crowd?"

"Get a fright, with me there to take care of you?"

"With you?" and I burst into a hearty laugh.

"Of course with me. There is nothing to laugh at, for I assure you I can be good company."

I laughed the more heartily that Pacheco's Andalusian accent amused me even more than his audacious proposal. His words came out mellowed by the
indolence of Southern speech, but without a tinge of
vulgarity.

He let me have my laugh out, then without losing
countenance calmly explained how feasible it was to
take a stroll through the Fair, returning to Madrid
about noon.

Ah, me! If I had but sealed my ears, how many
evils I might have avoided. Unfortunately the proposal began to tempt me. I remembered that the
Duchess had said the night before, "Go out to Saint
Isidro; it is so original and amusing."

After all, what harm could come of gratifying my
curiosity? I could hear mass just as well at the
Hermitage. With Pacheco by my side, no one would
venture to address me uncivilly. If we were seen,
was there any harm in our being together at that
hour in a public place? For that matter, what decent
person was I likely to meet at the Fair at ten o'clock
in the morning, a bull-fight day into the bargain?
The escapade offered little risk, the weather was so
inviting. In a word, if Pacheco were to press me a
little —

Pacheco did press me with polite persistence, till I
allowed myself to yield a smiling consent. Fatal
yielding! Scarcely had the "Yes" escaped me before we were plunged in a discussion of the best

means of transit. Pacheco argued for the horse-cars, as most appropriate to the spirit of the excursion; but I decided to take my own carriage, so that there might not be too much Bohemian flavor.

The stable was hard by, in Caballero de Gracia Street. Pacheco would take my message to the coachman and drive back to the house for me. Meanwhile I must go home to make some slight change in toilet, exchange prayer-book for fan and mantilla for hat. No sooner were these details decided on than Pacheco pressed my hand, and was off like a shot. Ten paces away he stopped to call out,

"In Caballero de Gracia Street, you said?"

"Yes, on the left side. The stable with the large entrance."

I felt in a hurry, too, and made the best of my way home. I had more to do than I confided to Pacheco, for of course a man needn't be told everything. My hair must be re-arranged, I must rub cold cream on my face, find a very fine handkerchief, select the new boots which fitted best, put on fresh gloves and slip a sachet of violet into my pocket — the only perfume which does not give me a headache. For, after all, Pacheco was a man of my own social rank, we were to pass several hours in close companionship, and I did not wish him to notice anything careless or unbecoming in my appearance. Any woman would feel as I did.

I reached home hot and flurried, rushed up the

steps, rang the bell furiously, tore into my dressing-room, and snatched off my mantilla before seating myself in front of the glass.

"Angela, my black straw, with plaid ribbons. My bronze boots. My checked parasol."

I could see that Diabla was devoured with curiosity. "Indeed," thought I, "this time you may take it out in wishing, my good girl. Curiosity is good for the appetite." But Diabla would not give up without an attempt. She began to question with a very innocent air.

"Will Madam return for breakfast?"

To avoid gratifying her, I replied indifferently,

"I am not sure, but in any case have it ready at eleven. If I am not in by one, you may clear away. But save me a chop and a cup of broth in any case. And don't forget my tea and toast."

While I was arranging my hair under the brim of my hat, I noticed on the mantel a pretty blue jar filled with heliotropes, gardenias and pinks.

"Who sent those flowers?" I asked.

"Major Pardo, Madam. Don Gabriel."

"Why didn't you tell me?"

"Madam was in such a hurry that I did not have time to think of anything."

Don Gabriel had sent me flowers before. I pinned a few blossoms in the front of my dress, tied on my veil, took a thin wrap over my arm, and told Diabla to pull out my draperies. Then I went to the window to see whether by any miracle the carriage had arrived. Not yet. Indeed, it was impossible. Ten minutes later I caught the sound of wheels at the corner of the street. I walked slowly through the hall, not to increase Diabla's suspicions, preserving my dignified mien until the door was fairly closed. Then I rushed down the staircase, reaching the entrance just as the berlin stopped, and Pacheco stepped out.

"The coachman must have hurried," said I.

"The coachman and your humble servant," replied he, holding the door open for me. "These hands helped to harness, and I fancy to wash the wheels, too."

I hurried in. Pacheco went round to the other door, to avoid passing in front of me, and seated himself beside me with an air of profound respect — the arch-hypocrite! We looked at each other undecidedly for a few seconds, then Pacheco asked in a submissive voice,

"Shall I tell him to take the Pradera road?"

"Yes, open the window and tell him."

He thrust his head out, and cried,

"To the Fair!"

The carriage rolled off, and Pacheco began immediately to talk.

"I see you have come prepared for sun and heat. I think you will need all you have brought."

I smiled, without answering, for, as was natural, I felt a little confused by the novelty of the position,

My escort did not lose heart.

"What beautiful flowers!" he continued. "Haven't you one to spare for me? Just a rosebud or a sprig of sweet basil?"

"You are not afraid to ask for what you want," murmured I, "but take this to keep you quiet."

I pulled out a gardenia, and offered it to him; but instead of taking it he adopted a most wheedling tone.

"I didn't dare to ask for so much. I should have been content with any leaf or bit you might have pulled off. A whole gardenia for me! I'm not prepared for such generosity, and I'm far too awkward to fasten it properly in the button-hole. Do you think your little fingers could?"

"I see! You were too modest to ask for a flower, and now you want me to pin it in for you. Well, turn a bit, so that I can get at your button-hole."

I fastened the toothpick stem of the gardenia with a pin from my belt. The perfume went to my head, together with another fine odor which proceeded doubtless from Pacheco's hair. I felt my cheeks getting red, and on glancing up my eyes met Pacheco's. Instead of thanking me in the usual way, he continued to regard me with a glance so expressive and inquiring that for the moment I almost repented of my sudden caprice. But since we had started —

I turned about, and looking out the window saw that we were entering the Toledo, from the Cebada Square. The carriage was surrounded by a crowd which streamed down towards the Pradera and at times almost stopped our progress. Among that throng in Sunday attire we observed here and there the bright colors of some embroidered Manila shawl, with fringe a third its width. The young girls displayed the frankest curiosity in examining the interior of the carriage. Once Pacheco put his head out of the window and said something to one of them.

"They take us for a newly married couple," he explained, turning back to me, "but don't blush deeper," he added, half to himself. "That gives the last touch to your beauty, and already — "

I pretended not to hear, and to change the subject called his attention to the picturesque aspect of the Toledo. What with the numerous taverns, the ambulant hardware stands, the old-fashioned shops and change houses, the old street looks just as it did in the time of Charles IV. But Pacheco, I observed, paid little heed to these details. Instead of looking at the curiosities of the most typical street in Madrid, he kept his eyes fixed secretly, but pertinaciously, on me, like one who is studying an unfamiliar physiognomy for the purpose of divining its owner's thoughts. I on my side managed to acquaint myself stealthily with every trait of my companion's countenance. I was struck more than ever with the apparent mixture of races which it exhibited. His coal-black hair and sunburnt skin contrasted oddly with his blue eyes and fair moustache.

"Was your mother an Englishwoman?" I asked. "I have heard that marriages between the English and Spanish are not infrequent on the Mediterranean coast."

"That is true, especially in Malaga; but every drop of my blood is Spanish."

I looked at him again, and realized the folly of my question. I called to mind something which I once heard from one of these scientists whom the Duchess invites to dinner when she has no one else to entertain her. He had denounced the popular belief that Spaniards are always dark. According to him, the blond type abounds in Spain. Not the Saxon fairness, to be sure, for the Spaniard is always more delicate and wiry, like the Arab steed. Indeed the Englishmen I have met are generally mountains of red flesh, suggestive of raw beef. Their necks look like slices of beets. Their foreheads are so white that they recall the "pale brow" of the romantic poets, and this beauty, well enough in a woman, seems effeminate in a man. What Englishman would you find with Pacheco's finely cut lips, his sunken temples, his spare, well-modelled neck? But back to my subject. I fear I recall with pleasure the attractions of the abandoned wretch.

How beautiful and gay the Toledo Bridge looked! It comes back to me like stage-setting at the Royal Theatre. On the bridge itself the people swarmed, and down towards the Pradera and the banks of the

Manzanares groups of young men, processions, family parties, were everywhere to be seen, for all the world like the scenes they paint on the tambourines. To my taste, certain structures, cathedrals, for instance, are most beautiful in solitude. But the Toledo Bridge, with its recesses, niches, or whatever those strange structures may be on each side, does not show to advantage without the noise and bustle of the Madrid throng — that crowd of young rowdies, butchers and draymen who seemed to have stepped out of Goya's canvases. The carriage was just turning into the Pradera road when I spied at the very end of the bridge such a curious old wine-skin shop. Along the front were hanging skins of all dimensions, from a fifteen-gallon size to a tiny thing you could carry in your pocket. Pacheco proposed that we buy a small skin, fill it with Valdepeñas and hang it out of the carriage window, "just to be in harmony with the spirit of the festival." But of course I rejected the plan with horror.

Who, I wonder, first called the banks of the Manzanares ugly and arid? Why do the newspapers forever crack jokes upon our poor river? And why did we allow the French writer (Dumas, I think) to live, after offering our stream the alms of a glass of water? I admit the Manzanares is not a cool, abundant river like our Mino or Sil, but yet it offers every now and then a fresh green spot. Its trees invite one to their shade, and pretty rustic bridges stretch

out between the washing establishments. Perhaps
this favorable impression of the river was due in a
measure to the fact that I was getting the better of
my first timidity, and rejoicing in my own courage.
Several circumstances contributed to complete my
satisfaction. My thin gray dress, dotted with tiny
red anchors, seemed appropriate to the informal
morning expedition. My straw hat became me — so
said the carriage mirror. The heat had not become
oppressive; my companion pleased me. At first the
lark had caused me some little uneasiness, but now it
was beginning to appear the most innocent affair in
the world, chiefly because I did not see a soul who
could recognize me. Nothing would have destroyed
my pleasure so much as to encounter some one of
the Sahagun circle, or some friendly neighbor in the
Royal Theatre. Acquaintances of that stamp would
be sure to pass uncomfortable criticisms on my little
excursion. There are always too many malicious
gossips about, ready to infer evil from the simplest
actions. It avails a woman little that her past life
has been blameless, if in the present she forget herself a single hour. (Too true! Don't I know that to
my cost? But I must go back.) The Pradera offered
a reassuring spectacle — the people here, there and
everywhere. If you saw a man in a sack-coat instead
of the national jacket, it was sure to be some lackey,
shop-boy, poor student, gardener or servant out of a
place, taking a day's pleasure. That is why, when we

got out to walk on account of the throng, Pacheco and I looked like some duke and his duchess incognito, attracted to the popular festival by curiosity, and betrayed by the elegance of their attire.

The motley spectacle pleased me by its novelty. As a fair it could not compete with those of Galicia, which are always held in some fresh spot, shaded by walnut and chestnut trees, with a brook near by, and the sanctuary on an adjoining hill. Saint Isidro's field comprises a series of bare hills — a dusty desert, where not a single peasant can be seen among the throng. The frequenters of the Fair are soldiers, rough women, tinkers, rowdies — a thievish, dirty race! Instead of vegetation, hundreds of booths for the sale of trumpery which is never seen except at the Fair. Whistles adorned with silver paper and astonishing roses; Virgins daubed with cobalt, vermilion and emerald green; medals and scapularies in colors equally vivid; all kinds of crockery and earthenware; coarsely-made figures of bull-fighters; strange jars; caricatures of Martos, Sagasta or Castelar; figures of Saint Isidro, and beside them certain little statuettes which really were too — Heaven help us! It was best to pretend not to see them.

Even without the sun to melt our brains, and the dust to choke us, the medley of staring metallic colors was enough to make my head swim. I felt that to look longer would make my eyes ache. The pyramids of oranges began to look a mass of flame. The

dates shone like deep carbuncles.   The roasted beans
and peanuts glistened like grains of gold.   The flower-
stands blazed with brilliant carnations, yellow, blood
red and deep rose, like sunset clouds.   But the per-
fumes of that wilderness of flowers could not dominate
the odor of fritters frying in oil — the most nauseat-
ing smell in the whole world, I believe.   As I have
said, there was no color which did not agonize the
eye.   The uniform of the soldiers, the girls' gay
shawls, the bright blue of the sky, the yellow of the
soil, the swings striped with ochre and indigo.   And
then the music!   The scratching of guitars and the
abominable thud of the street-piano grinding out the
"Quickstep from Cadiz" in a dozen different directions.

Let no one maliciously imagine that I had forgotten
about mass.   We tried to force a way through the
crowd to the Hermitage, which was opened every few
minutes to the devout.   But the crowd was so dense,
so determined, so vulgar and so evil-smelling that had
I persisted in forcing my way in, they would have
brought me out either fainting or dead.   Pacheco
used his fists and elbows freely, but merely with the
result of increasing the jam, and calling forth the
most infamous oaths and blasphemies.   At last I
pulled him by the sleeve.

"Let us go back," said I.   "I give it up for an
impossibility."

When once again in breathable atmosphere, I sighed
penitently, "God forgive me ; no mass to-day !"

"Never mind," said Pacheco. "I will hear a mass for you, even if they chant all the Gregorians. That will clear off your account."

"Yes; Father Urdax will clear off my account as soon as he lays eyes on me!" thought I to myself, as I rubbed my shoulder, which was suffering from a ferocious nudge from one of the Caffres.

CHAPTER IV

I HAD thought Don Diego rather reserved and melancholy in the carriage, but as soon as we set foot in the Fair he became exceedingly loquacious, justifying his reputation for good company. Holding my arm fast, so that the human tide might not separate us, he improved the opportunity to make jokes on everything he saw. The point of his jests lay in his accent and expression, in his quickness to catch every shade of humor, rather than in his words ; and this is true of Andalusian wit in general.

The worst of it was that as we appeared to be the only respectable persons in the Fair, and Pacheco had a word for everybody, we were soon surrounded by a train of beggars, phenomenons, ragged children, gypsies and fritter-fryers. My companion's impulse was to buy everything offered him, from scapularies to big earthen jars, and he purchased right and left until I made a formal protest.

"I shall be angry if you buy another thing."

"Zounds ! that settles it. No more purchases, then. The next one who asks me to buy will get his pay in fisticuffs, d'ye hear? Has my lady other orders for her slave ? "

"I would give anything for five minutes in the shade."

"To prison with you, then, for compromising a lady. Shall I call the police, and have you sent to a cool cell?"

Now that I consider the situation in cold blood I see how improper it was for me to converse with Don Diego in that tone of familiarity after three quarters of an hour's walk with him through the Saint Isidro. Perhaps Don Gabriel is right after all. Perhaps there is something in our sun, in the air and hubbub of a popular festival which operates on body and mind like a heady wine; which breaks down from the first moment the breastwork of reserve which we women build up with such labor, to be our safeguard against dangerous familiarities. Be that as it may, I must have felt the beginning of that dangerous intoxication when I replied gayly,

"In prison or anywhere, if the sun is shut out. I feel so queer, almost as if I were going to faint."

" Do you feel really ill?" asked Pacheco, seriously, and with an appearance of lively interest.

" No; not ill, but tired and feverish. I can scarcely see plain."

Pacheco burst out laughing and said in my ear,

"I can guess what is the matter with you, without being a mind-reader, either. You are suffering from inanition."

"What in the world is that?" asked I, surprised at the queer word.

"To use a less scientific term — hunger," replied

Pacheco. "And you are not the only one. Severe pangs have been racking me this half hour, and no wonder; it must be near mid-day."

"Perhaps you are right. One is apt to feel faint about meal times. Well, we have seen the Fair; let us return to the city, and breakfast at my house, if that suits you."

"My dear Marchioness, don't you see that we are in a regular town here? Do let us breakfast together at one of the inns about, for I can assure you that the inns are —"

Pacheco threw a kiss in the air to express the superlative quality of the Saint Isidro inns.

Tired and demoralized as I had become, the idea frightened me. I thought it indecorous, and saw at a glance the risks and difficulties of the plan. But at the same time, in my secret soul, these very dangers lent the bold scheme a delicious charm — the attraction which always hovers over the unknown and forbidden. Did I fear Pacheco to be a forward fellow, likely to take liberties without encouragement? Certainly not; and for that matter it was my business to see that he should get no encouragement. What a good time I should lose by refusing. Goodness, what would Pardo say to this adventure? But if he knows nothing about it? While these thoughts were shooting through my brain, I was refusing aloud, with great resolution. No; it was out of the question. Back to Madrid at once.

Pacheco stood his ground. Instead of taking my refusal seriously, he made a joke of it. With jests and compliments, drawling out his words more than ever, he vowed he would fall an inanimate mass at my feet, if he were obliged to wait twenty minutes longer for food.

"I will go down on my knees in the dust," cried he. "Oh, for a 'yes' from that rosy mouth. We shall eat the greatest breakfast of the nineteenth century. Propriety be hanged! Do you think I am going to tell the Duchess of Sahagun about our little lark? In charity, a breakfast for a starving man."

I could not help showing a smile, and then I had the weakness to say,

"But what about the carriage, which is waiting yonder all this time?"

"It won't take a minute to let the coachman know he is to put the horses up, or if there is no stable near, to drive back to Madrid, and return at sunset. Wait a moment while I find some one to take the message, for I can't leave my lamb here alone, to be devoured by the wolves."

A policeman who was patrolling the Fair must have overheard us, for he approached at this juncture, and offered his services in a respectful tone, in great contrast to his rough way of ordering the idlers to move on.

"I will take the message," said he with an amiable smile. "Where is the carriage, and what is the coachman's name?"

"Why, this man is from my Galicia," cried I, as

soon as I heard his accent. "What part do you come from?"

"I live about three leagues from Lujo," replied he, his eyes sparkling with pleasure at meeting some one from his own province.

On the instant I was struck with a sudden fear. Suppose he should know me, through Diabla? But my dread proved unfounded, for he said no more. To get rid of him, I hastened to point out the carriage.

"You see the berlin with red wheels, and the young coachman with side-whiskers and green livery? No; farther along. The eighth in the line."

"Yes, Madam, I see it now."

"Tell the coachman," put in Pacheco, "to go straight back to Madrid, and return towards evening, and wait for us at the same place. Do you understand?"

I noticed that my companion took the policeman's hand and pressed it with great effusion. But it could not have been this honor which painted such joy on the latter's countenance, for I saw him close his right hand, and slip it into his pocket. He left us with the classic formula of thanks on his lip, "A hundred years to you!"

We were free from the incumbrance of the carriage. I leaned more heavily on Don Diego's arm, and he pressed mine closer, as if ratifying a contract.

"Let us begin to climb the hill," he said. "Take a good breath. Lean on me."

The sun by this time was encamped in the midst of the heavens, pouring down flames and shooting forth rays of dazzling light. No breeze stirred, and we inhaled with every breath an atmosphere of clayey dust. I scanned the horizon in search of the promised inn, which would at least provide a roof between me and that tropical sun. Not a sign of any sort of large building was to be seen before or behind us. The only solid walls in sight were those of the Hermitage, within which the dead slept in peace, ignorant of the follies committed by the living outside. I shook my sunshade at Pacheco.

"And that fine inn of yours? May I inquire how long we are to wander about, looking for it?"

"Inn?" he rejoined, as if the question surprised him. "Did you ask for an inn? The fact is—" "Why, confound it, I can't make out where it is."

"Certainly you are a strange fellow! Didn't you assure me that the hill abounded in the most palatial inns in the universe? And now you are leading me this wild-goose chase up hill and down dale in the broiling sun! You might ask some one, at least."

"Hello, friend!"

A snub-nosed, pallid, vicious-looking fellow in a high silk cap and tight trousers turned round. A perfect example of the rat type. A fellow to make you tremble just by his way of slouching along.

"Is there any kind of good inn about here?" asked Pacheco, handing him a cigar.

"Thanks.   As for inns, why, of course there are some places — any one could show you a dozen. But a nice house for swells, with oysters and fixings — I don't think you'll find any, but perhaps you may."

"There are none but little lunch booths, that is clear," said Pacheco, in a low, disappointed tone.

On observing his evident discomfort, an instinct of humorous contradiction which develops itself in women under such circumstances made me declare myself satisfied.   And really, the chance of break-fasting in an open tent did not displease me.   It was so characteristic.   It was more novel and unexpected, less clandestine and dangerous, than our original plan.   What risk could there be in a tent, open on three sides, and free to the public?   It looked just as innocent as taking a glass of beer in an open-air café.

CHAPTER V

CONVINCED that there was no inn of any kind, we looked about for some booth less vulgar and unattractive than the others. Near the top of the hill we spied a large one of clean appearance. Unlike the neighboring stands it displayed none of the absurd signs, such as,

"Saint Isidro's favorite dishes."

"Here you can get the earth in meat and drink."

"Café Effulgence! Periwinkles and tripe!"

At the entrance (there was no door) stood a pleasant-faced girl, with a nickel stiletto thrust through her pug. Not a soul was to be seen inside the tent. The six clean tables were scoured white, and the establishment had the appearance of an army tent, the walls being of canvas, and the roof formed of pieces of matting stretched over narrow beams. Of the three divisions within, the smallest, at the back, contained a little stove, the next served as a sort of pantry, and the third was the dining-room. We thought best not to pry into the mysteries of the two smaller compartments lest our appetites should suffer. The floor consisted simply of the yellow sand which forms the whole arid hill of Saint Isidro. The dirty old woman who appeared and began to scour a

table had only to stoop down to obtain the chief
material for her cleansing process.

We seated ourselves away from the entrance, on a
wooden bench which could boast no other back than
the canvas of the tent. The girl with her nickel
stiletto and gummed spit-curls hurried up to take our
orders. She felt that we were liberal patrons, and
perhaps she suspected something else about us, for
she smiled at me so knowingly that I felt myself turn
crimson. Her smile said plainer than words, "A
happy couple, these two. What brings them billing
and cooing to Saint Isidro? Better for them to stay
in their own nest, I think; for nest they have beyond
a doubt." Reading these thoughts in the girl's eyes,
I adopted a most reserved and dignified air, address-
ing Pacheco as one addresses a friend who can never
be anything more. But the precaution, far from
throwing dust in the officious girl's eyes, appeared to
confirm her suspicions. She began with the usual
question,

"What will you order?"

"What can you give us?" retorted Pacheco. "Out
with your whole list, my beauty, and the lady will
choose."

"We keep about everything. Do you wish a hearty
breakfast?"

"The heartier the better."

"Then, for the first course, omelet or scrambled
eggs?"

"Scrambled eggs. Have you bacon, too?"

"We have ham, and veal cutlets — fine ones."

"Fish?"

"Not fresh fish, but if you care for canned, we have pickled bream and sardines."

"No oysters?"

"No, Madam; we can't sell many high-priced things here. The customers mostly call for tripe, periwinkles and Valdepeñas and chops."

"Have you made up your mind?" said I, turning to Pacheco.

"Shall I order? Well then, bring us everything you mentioned, my pretty blossom; ham, eggs, cutlets, sardines — but first of all a bottle of Manzanillo, clean glasses and olives."

"And what shall I bring first — the cutlets?"

"No, my beauty; the eggs first, and then ham, sardines and cutlets, and cheese for dessert, if you have any."

"I should say we had, Flemish cheese and Villalón, as well as almonds, sweet cakes, roasted hazelnuts —"

"We shall breakfast better than the Pope's Nuncio!" exclaimed Pacheco, rubbing his hands, and I thought so too. Those "barbarities," as the Major called them, had sharpened my appetite, and my good humor sensibly increased on finding myself sheltered from the terrible sun.

It is true that the tent offered no better protection

than an umbrella might afford at mid-day in an open
field.   The sun could not get at our skulls, indeed,
but it filtered through on every side, steeping us in
fiery vapor.   Between the imperfectly joined mats on
the roof, through the canvas sides, and above all by
the entrance, the heat entered in surges, in torrents.
And not alone the heat, but the swell of the human
sea without, the cries, disputes, songs, coarse laughter,
the scraping of guitars and lutes, and that infernal
quickstep "Viva España!" thumped out by the mechanical pianos.

The waitress with the stiletto was placing the Manzanillo "Superfino," and the relishes on the table,
when through the opening there appeared a dishevelled
woman with eyes like live coals.   She wore a cotton
skirt with stiffly starched ruffles, and across her breast
was tied a faded woollen shawl through the folds of
which appeared a baby's head.   The woman planted
herself in front of us, one hand on her hip, the other
flourishing in strange gesticulations.   How the child
was supported I could not imagine.

"In the name of the Father, the Son and the Holy
Ghost," she began.   "Where the name of God goes
nothing evil can follow.   Pretty lady, you would
give a great deal to know what I can read in your
little hand."

"Bless me," cried I, overjoyed, "this is a gypsy
fortune-teller!"

"Shall I send her away?   Does she annoy you?"

" On the contrary, she amuses me immensely. Just
wait and hear what ridiculous nonsense she will spin
out. Here, Gypsy, tell my fortune quick ; I'm dying
of curiosity."

" Give me your hand, my pretty lady, and cross
the palm with silver."

Pacheco handed her a *peseta*, and having uncorked
the Manzanillo and asked for another glass, he filled
it with wine and offered it to the Egyptian dame.
Then began an exchange of quips and jokes, well sus-
tained on both sides. It was easy to see that they
were children of the same soil, with the same facility
of utterance, the same inexhaustible flow of words.
When the gypsy had finished her glass of wine I was
induced to drink one also, for the clear liquid tempted
my thirsty lips. Superfine Manzanillo ! Everything
was superfine in that place. The blessed wine tasted
of wicker, of alum, of Beelzebub's horns ; but as, after
all, it was a liquid, and I felt thirsty enough to drink
up the Manzanares, I presently drank a second glass
which Pacheco had poured out for me. But far from
feeling refreshed, it seemed to me that a jet of pul-
verized solar heat had been shot into my veins. I
could feel it sparkling out of my eyes, and burning
out in my cheeks. I smiled at Pacheco, and then
became confused, for he paid my glance with one of
uncomfortable length.

" What charming blue eyes the man has," thought I.
He had taken off his hat. His handsome suit of

rich, soft gray became him admirably.   From time to
time he wiped his moist forehead with the finest of
handkerchiefs, disordering his silky black hair.   But
the disorder increased his charm.   When he laughed
his white teeth lighted up his whole face, making his
dark skin browner by contrast, or rather more sunburnt, for a white line at the collar showed the true
color of his complexion.

"Your hand, my pretty lady," repeated the gypsy.

I stretched it out, and the prophetess took it in her
own.   Pacheco looked at the two hands.

"What a contrast!" he murmured, not as though
paying a compliment, but rather like a man talking
to himself.

And really, vanity apart, I must say that the gypsy's
hand beside mine looked like an ugly lump of smoked
beef, and her silver-plated ring with a prodigious false
emerald only heightened the coppery color of her
claw.   Now, my hand is rather small, white and well
cared for, and with its ornament of pearl, sapphire and
diamond rings it certainly did offer a strange contrast.
The dame pretended to trace the lines on my palm,
while she muttered something which passed for a
spell.   Then she began to reel off an infinity of those
safe conventional prophecies which fit all cases as the
old oracles did.   All was well emphasized with im-
pressive winks and nods.

"One thing I discover in this little hand; something of importance will happen very soon, but nobody

suspects it. You are going on a journey, but this is not a misfortune. It will turn out for the satisfaction of every one. A letter is coming which will make you very happy. Certain persons wish you ill, and are scheming to work you evil, but their wickedness shall fall on their own heads. A certain individual is over head and ears in love with you " (at this point she fixed her burning eyes on Pacheco), "and some one who loves you is going to give you an invitation soon. You are a loving nature, but you can get angry as a mountain lioness, and then let them beware of vexing you ! Gentleness and devotion are the means to win your heart, but when you are angry, you would think nothing of throwing yourself into the Bay of Cadiz. You are hiding an affection in your breast. Not a living soul knows it ; even to you yourself your heart is a sealed book. It is a secret yet, but a star will shoot from heaven, and you will be struck with amazement. Now you are like a bird that flies without knowing on which tree it is to alight."

She would have been talking still, I believe, if we had not interrupted her. Her chatter amused me, for in these vague, diffuse tirades there is always something which responds to our own feelings, hopes or aspirations.

Pacheco watched me attentively, ready to dismiss the prophetess the moment her talk wearied me. Seeing that the girl with the nickel stiletto was bringing the scrambled eggs I pulled my hand away, and he sent the

gypsy off.   Before stepping out again into the dusty
road she begged a trifle more for her pickaninny.

We were beginning to despatch the appetizing
medley of dishes and taste the bottle of sherry when
another figure appeared at the entrance and approached
our table, mumbling the well-known formula,

"In the name of the Father, the Son and the —"

"We are in luck," cried Pacheco ; "here's another
gypsy."

"Of course," muttered the girl, with aristocratic
disdain.   "You gave money and wine to the other,
and now it is over the whole hill.   We shall have the
whole Fair here before long."

Pacheco threw the newcomer some coppers, and
poured out a glass of sherry for her.

"Drink to our good healths, and be off," said he.

"I will tell your fortunes for nothing !   You don't
know what good luck you are missing !"

"No, no," whispered I.   "She will come out with
the same pack of nonsense as the first one.   Enough
is as good as a feast.   Send her away peaceably."

"Drink your wine, sweetheart, and then — skip !"
said Pacheco pleasantly, in a tone of familiar command.

Convinced that nothing more could be obtained,
the woman gulped down the sherry, wiped her mouth
on the back of her hand, and made off, carrying the
inevitable pickaninny, which was suspended from her
neck in the same mysterious way, and looked like a
mite in the cheese.

"They all have babies, it seems," said I to the waitress.

"Yes, indeed, Madam," replied she in the *blasé* tone of an old stager. "That is to say, they all carry them round. But the gypsies are the greatest cheats! Those babies no more belong to them than they do to me. They hire the poor things of other wretches as bad as themselves, and Heaven knows how they use the little innocents. The Fair is overrun with that kind of vermin, more's the pity."

"Do you live here?" asked I, to draw her out. "Are you not afraid of losing to-day's gain and to-morrow's provisions while you sleep?"

"Madam, we have to sleep with one eye open, that's a fact. But you see we keep a café near the Plaza Mayor, and just come here to get up hot suppers at night."

Evidently she was giving herself airs, wishing to impress us as being vastly superior to the other restaurant keepers about. Meanwhile we were making great progress with the eggs and ham. Presently another shadow darkened the doorway, and in came a bare-armed girl in a striped silk shawl and high ball comb, carrying a great jar full of carnations and roses. She addressed Pacheco in a low, wheedling drawl,

"Buy my flowers to give to your pretty lady!"

At the same time four soldiers entered, young boisterous hussars, who called loudly for beer and soda water. Their sabres clinked gayly, and their blue and yellow uniforms furnished a joyous bit of color to break the monotony of the white tent.

What strange virtue dwells in Manzanillo and sherry, especially when they are well adulterated! At another time, what should I have thought of breakfasting in the same room with common soldiers? The very suggestion would have sent me into hysterics. As it was, my notions of propriety were overturned; the company of those men actually gave me pleasure, and I laughed at their jokes with all my heart. Observing my good humor Pacheco joined the hussars, and treated them to sherry and other delicacies; so that we were not simply lunching in the same room, but were actually fraternizing with those low strangers.

When one is in good humor nothing seems amiss. I praised the food, and called the flower-girl a Sala study, whereupon Pacheco immediately seized the whole bunch of flowers and threw them in my lap, crying out,

"Pin them all on — every one!"

I did so, making the whole front of my waist one great sweet-scented bouquet. After that I remember that I nearly died laughing at a vulgar quarrel which drifted in to us through the canvas walls, and at Pacheco's chaff with the soldiers.

The sunlight of the doorway was again cut off by the entrance of a ragged beggar. Not content with the bestowal of liberal alms, Pacheco drew the fellow into conversation, and made him relate his adventures

— a string of lies, I presume. We listened, however, as though it were gospel, and my companion insisted he should sing for us to the guitar. In vain the wretch swore that he had never touched the instrument, that he knew nothing more than a few *coplas;* we never let him go until he had promised to fetch us some good singer who would give us *seguidillas* and *peteneras* to our hearts' content. Fortunately, he did not keep his promise.

All this entertained me more than a play, and disposed me to do full justice to the chops and champagne. I realized that my eyes were shooting fire, and that a match might have been lighted at my cheeks; but I felt none of the lethargy which I supposed preceded intoxication. A highly agreeable animation possessed me, loosened my tongue, excited my senses, quickened my wit and filled my heart with joy. What reassured me above all as to my condition was that I felt the necessity of maintaining a certain decorum and reserve in speech and action. And really I did preserve my dignity, avoiding every word and movement which might appear equivocal, but of course without checking my gaiety, ceasing to praise the sauces or to show myself less jovial than the occasion demanded. For, after all, would it not have been odd if I had sat there like a death's head at a feast?

CHAPTER VI

Pacheco added fuel to the flames, taking care that my plate should never remain empty, nor my glass either. He suited his humor to mine as if he were some master of ceremonies charged to provide constant entertainment for a visiting potentate.

Alas! cost what it will, I must give this agreeable devil his due. Tête-à-tête with my conscience I must admit that animated, joking, jovial as he was, and moreover my accomplice in a glaring infringement of decorum, Pacheco never permitted himself to cross the line of good taste, by indulging in familiarity of word or action. The gallantry permissible under ordinary circumstances would have been uncourteous and presuming in my strange and critical position. I realized this, and, to tell the truth, half feared to suffer some of those veiled impertinences which cannot be resented in words, and destroy all sense of enjoyment.

Without Pacheco's delicacy of feeling the situation in which I had so thoughtlessly placed myself might have become very ridiculous for me. But although he loaded the waitress, the flower-girl and even the scrub-woman with the most extravagant compliments, to me he never breathed a word of flattery. It is

true that I found his blue eyes devouring me on the
sly; but they turned away as soon as they met mine.
Everything he said to me was simple, serious and
respectful in the extreme. Looking back now, I can
fancy this reserve kept up to inspire me with confidence. Holy Virgin! how dear I have bought that
respectful courtesy!

Suddenly a little yellow gypsy appeared at my
elbow, so quietly that we could not imagine how she
had entered. She looked to be about thirteen. Any
artist would have been glad to paint her just as she
stood, with her blue-black hair knotted and secured
by an odd horn comb, and a blood-red carnation droop-
ing by her left ear. Her eyes and teeth contrasted
sharply with her dusky skin, her forehead was flat as
a viper's, and her bare arms looked like two yellowish-
green snakes. In the whining tone of the others of
her tribe, she began the well-known formula,

"In the name of the Father, the Son — "

This time our waitress roused herself, and throwing
her fine-lady airs to the winds, she showed herself a
true daughter of the people, and of the most free-
spoken type.

"How dare you come here, you gad-about baggage?
Can't decent folks eat their victuals in peace? Snake's
nest of gypsies! Sweep one away, and another drops
on your head. How did this abomination get in, I
wonder? Make tracks like lightning, or you'll get
such a crack as you never felt in all your life! I'll

dress you down, so that you'll have no tongue left to tell of it!"

The gypsy darted off like a rocket. But two seconds later the canvas behind me parted, and we saw a foaming mouth, bristling with sharp teeth, and a bronzed fist which the gypsy shook as she bellowed,

"Jade! Castaway! She-devil!" (We are obliged to soften the language.) "May poisonous adders sting you! May your hair drop out till you are as bald as your carrion grandmother!"

So far she had proceeded in her rosary of curses, when the waitress, enraged at the impudent challenge, seized a saucepan, and rushed forward, like a wild creature, to brain her enemy. In the act, her elbow knocked over a bottle of sherry on the chimney-piece, and the wine ran out. This accident diverted her attention. She forgot her anger and began to laugh gaily, exclaiming,

"The Virgin be praised! Wine on the mantel, a sure sign of a wedding." I suppose the little gypsy took advantage of the opportunity to make her escape.

Nothing else worthy of record occurred during the breakfast, but my clear recollection of all these details shows that I had my wits about me. We sipped the last drop of champagne and drank a cup of muddy coffee. Pacheco paid the reckoning, feed in a Christian spirit, and we set off for a walk about the Fair. I noticed an unusual lightness in my limbs, as though my body had lost its weight, and I was gliding over the earth, rather than walking on it.

As we stepped outside the sun quite dazzled me, although it was no longer in the zenith. But at that hour — half-past three or four in the afternoon — the sun's rays are fiercest, and the very earth seemed cracking open with the heat. I thought the crowd three times greater and twenty times noisier than in the morning. No sooner had we joined the throng than an extraordinary fancy took possession of me. I believed, really believed, that I had fallen into a sea — a fiery sea which boiled and bubbled. I floated in a tiny boat no bigger than a nutshell, up on one wave, down on the next! Yes, I was certainly on the ocean, a prey to all the anguish of incipient sea-sickness!

Far from dissipating, my illusion grew stronger as I walked about on Pacheco's arm. No doubt about it. I was in the midst of a watery gulf. The innumerable sounds of voices, quarrels, oaths, prayers, guitars, hurdy-gurdies, street pianos, all mingled in a single noise: the dull roar of the ocean breaking on the reefs! Afar off, the swings flying giddily through the air looked to my sick brain like launches and feluccas, rocked by the waves. What despair I felt to find myself on the high-seas! I clung to Pacheco's arm as I remember clinging to the man's neck at the sea-baths, to keep myself from being swept away by the waters. Panic seized me, but I dared not confess

my fear.   Suppose Pacheco should laugh at me,
secretly or openly, when I told him that I was fast
becoming seasick ?

A new spectacle detained us a few minutes.   Two
women fighting, but in a strange fashion.   These
Amazonic combats are usually accompanied by vocif-
erations and insults, but this was quite different.   A
young woman was roasting peas over a small stove
when another, passing by, overturned the whole affair
with her skirts.   The toaster's face assumed such an
expression of ferocity as I had never seen before on
human countenance   Quick as a flash she seized the
pan, and threw herself like an infuriated tigress on
the other woman, striking her a tremendous blow
full in the face with the iron handle.   Blood spurted
from the cut, but the victim did not even groan.   She
turned round, grasped her assailant's hair and pulled
out a good handful by the roots, at the same time
digging her nails into the toaster's neck.   The two
Amazons fell to the ground, rolling among the pieces
of the stove and the cooking utensils.   A group
quickly formed about them, but no one attempted to
separate the two women   Lying at full length they
continued to struggle, silent, pallid as death ; the one
with her ear torn, the other with blood streaming
down her face, and one eye half out.   Several soldiers
stood near, laughing violently, and roaring out inde-
cent compliments to the unhappy creatures who were
tearing each other to pieces.

My giddiness disappeared for a moment before that horrible sight. I thought of Pardo and his theory of Spanish barbarism. But the idea soon fled, giving place to another delusion. The two combatants transformed themselves into monster fishes, like dolphins or sharks. They flapped their prickly tails, and snapped their horrid jaws in the effort to destroy each other. With the fancy of a marine combat, back came my nausea. I had to drag Pacheco away.

"Let us go, for the sake of heaven. They are killing each other."

Don Diego inquired if the sight made me feel ill, adding that we might omit the panoramas and side-shows, if that were the case. I replied sharply that I felt perfectly well, and disposed to examine all the curiosities of the Fair. We visited several tents, saw a dwarf, a two-headed calf and a woman with four legs. She looked bright, and was rigged out in a very low-necked blue silk, trimmed with cotton lace. The poor thing laughed convulsively as she showed us the double leg springing from each knee. In that little shed my ocean delusion swelled stronger than ever. On the left side a series of peep-holes was arranged for a cosmorama. I took them to be the ports of the ship, and was unshaken in the belief, even when I saw the Arc de l'Etoile and other foreign buildings through them. The architectural perspectives looked out of drawing, and all the outlines appeared blurred, as if a veil of tossing waves obstructed the view.   I took the concave and convex mirrors, which distorted my face so queerly, for pools of salt-water, and, gracious heavens! how sick it all made me feel!   Suddenly a dreadful thought crossed my mind.   What if all these marine fancies were simply and solely — inebriety, to put it mildly? But I drank very little wine, I felt so well at table.

"Holy Virgin!" thought I in terror.   "If Pacheco should suspect!   I must keep up appearances, get back to Madrid as soon as possible."

But the motion of the carriage would surely prove the last straw, and betray my true condition.   Air, air!   Away from the stifling crowd!

Either Pacheco divined my thoughts or he felt himself the need of coolness and quiet, for he stooped down and said with affectionate deference,

"The heat is becoming intolerable.   Don't you think so?   Suppose we get away from here?   The Pradera looks cool.   Let us walk down to the Alameda; it is more retired."

"Just as you please," replied I, feigning indifference, but feeling Heaven open before me at his proposition.

CHAPTER VII

We left the shed and walked down the hill towards the Alameda, pushed and propelled continually by the waves of that human sea, which was becoming more turbulent as night approached. At one time the press was so great that Pacheco had to drag me through the crowd by main force. My temples throbbed, my heart beat violently, my eyes clouded and a cold sweat beaded my forehead. I scarcely knew what was passing around me. As we were forcing our way through one group, a terrible sight just in front stopped us. We saw the deadly gleam of a pair of knives cleaving the air in search of human flesh. They were those weapons popularly called "*lenguas de vaca*" ("cows' tongues"), with their motto, "If this viper stings you, there is no remedy in the doctor's shop." I saw the soldiers' weapons glisten, and clubs raised. All the air was filled with vile words and horrible blasphemies. Dumb with terror, I clung to Pacheco's arm.

"Come this way," he whispered. "Don't be afraid. I am armed."

He showed me the muzzle of his revolver, protruding from his pocket. The sight of it only redoubled my terror, and I made every effort to get away from

that dangerous locality. This proved the less difficult that every one else was rushing to the scene of
the fray. We retreated quickly to the Alameda, a
comparatively retired spot; but even there my sea
delusion followed me. The carriages, carts and om-
nibuses — every kind of vehicle drawn up there, waiting for the returning pleasure-seekers — all appeared
to me under the form of boats anchored in a bay or
drawn up on the beach. They were steam-boats,
with side wheels, or pleasure-craft, with masts and
rigging. I could smell the smoke and the tar. Truly,
my sea delusion was of the strongest.

"Let us go over there, by the river, where it is
quiet," I entreated. "Where it is cool, and not a
soul will disturb us. All these people make me —"
A last remnant of caution held me back, and I hastily
corrected myself. "They tire me so!"

"Away from everybody? That will be difficult
to-day. Look." And he pointed towards the meadow.

Over the green field, on the bare hill-tops, surged the
same dense mass of human beings. The same confusion of bright colors, the same dizzy flight of swings and
swirl of dancers greeted the eye in every direction.

"Over yonder appears to be a quiet spot," said I.

To reach the place I had indicated we found it
necessary to climb over a rather high fence. Pacheco
vaulted across, and held out his arms to me from the
other side. I jumped down with surprising ease.
The laws of gravitation seemed suspended in my

favor, for my body felt light as a feather. I could have capered like a tight-rope dancer. Alas! stability did not equal lightness. A mere finger-push would have sent me rolling like a ball.

We crossed a ploughed field, jumping from furrow to furrow; then by solitary paths reached a tiny house which stood bathing its feet in the Manzanares. How restful to be there almost alone, with the noise of the Fair nearly lost in the distance! A charming little breeze blew fresh from the water, and dusk was descending. Heaven be praised, yonder we leave the stormy ocean, with its thundering waves, its sheets of spray, its cruel reefs! Here am I on the peaceful shore of a little cove, where the water just ripples up in tiny wavelets, which die out on the sand without disturbing any one.

Still a sea delusion, even here! If this continues —

A poorly dressed woman with two ragged children appeared on the threshold. The children very politely brought me a chair, and Pacheco seated himself on a pile of logs near me. I felt unspeakable content as I sat there and watched the burning sun bury its last red splendor in the waters of the Manzanares. But far from believing that I was looking at the river, I thought that expanse of water to be the Bay of Vigo. The house, too, had been transformed, I fancied, into a light launch which rocked me with almost imperceptible motion. Pacheco sat in the stern, holding the rudder. I reclined beside him, my elbow on his knee, my head resting on his shoulder, and my eyes closed, the better to enjoy the fresh sea breeze which fanned my face.   Holy Virgin, what bliss !   Hence to Heaven !

I opened my eyes.   What a shock !   I sat in the very position I have described.   Pacheco, holding me as tenderly as though I were a sick child, was fanning me with my own fan !

The uneasiness, the unspeakable fatigue which suddenly seized on me gave me no time to reflect on my singular situation.   I felt something like a hook, which seemed to be dragging my stomach up through my throat.   Raising my hands to my head, I gasped,

"Let me ashore; stop the boat !   I'm seasick — dying !   In the Virgin's name, let me ashore !"

After that I lost sight of the bay, the green, foaming sea, the crinkly waves.   I no longer heard the northeast wind blowing ; no longer smelt the tar.   I was conscious, as if between dreams, that they lifted me, and carried me away.   Were we disembarking ? I heard half sentences which conveyed no meaning to my mind.   "Poor thing, she's had a turn !   This way, sir.   Certainly, there is a good bed, and everything." Apparently they had brought me to dry land, for I experienced a tremendous relief, as if a giant hand had smashed an iron band which compressed my sides, impeding respiration.   I sighed and opened my eyes.

It was a lucid interval such as occurs in attacks of frenzy.   I understood all that had happened.   There was no sea, no vessel — nothing but an alcoholic delusion. The *terra firma* was the hostess's great bed; the iron band, my corset which they had loosened. If I did not die of shame on the spot, it was only because Pacheco was not to be seen in the room, no one but the woman, tall, dark and affable, outdoing herself in offers of assistance.

"Nothing, thank you," I said. "Quiet and a darkened room are all I need. Yes, I will call if I need anything. I feel better already, and will try to sleep."

The woman drew the blinds, through which a faint gleam of sunlight entered, and went gently out. An invincible drowsiness overpowered me; I could not move hand or foot. Soon the dark and quiet began to have their effect. My head and heart felt much better, but at the same time my old tormenting delusion returned. I remember thinking, "How comfortable it is in this cabin, and how smooth the sea must be, for the boat doesn't even rock!"

I have often heard it claimed that if our eyes are closed, and some person looks fixedly at us, an inexplicable force will compel us presently to raise our eyelids. I can declare this to be true, from personal experience. In the midst of my stupor my eyelids began to twitch, and a curious inquietude intimated to me the presence of some one in the room. Half opening my eyes, I saw to my great astonishment the waters of the ocean. Not the green and lead colored Cantabrian waters, but the clear blue of the

Mediterranean — Pacheco's eyes, as you may well imagine. He stood near me, and when he met my glance he stooped and delicately arranged the folds of my skirt so as to cover my feet.

"How are you feeling? Well enough to venture up?" he murmured, or at least something of the sort, for I cannot be sure of the words. What I am sure of is that I stretched out both hands with sudden and extraordinary affection. At that moment I thought I was abandoned in the midst of a wide gulf, in imminent danger of drowning if Pacheco did not succeed in coming to my assistance. He took my outstretched hands, pressed them warmly, felt my pulse and stroked my forehead gently. How much good that careful, firm pressure did me! It seemed to replace and lubricate the jarred hinges of my brain. I pressed his hand in return. One becomes so silly and dependent in these — in such abnormal situations, and I felt hungry for caresses, just like a little child. Every one knows about the sentimental stage of intoxication. In my condition I felt so anxious that he should pity me that I was ready to weep, just for the pleasure of being consoled.

At the head of the bed stood a dirty cane chair. Pacheco seated himself in it, and laid his face close to mine on the hard pillow. What did he whisper in my ear? I do not know, but it must have been something soothing and flattering, for I continued to press his hand with convulsive force, smiling and

half closing my eyes. I fancied that we were floating in the skiff, and heard the waves strike harmoni-
ously, clap! clap! on the boat's sides. I felt a warm
breath on my cheek, and a velvet contact, like the
passage of butterfly-wings. Loud steps resounded.
I opened my eyes and saw the dark woman — the
inn-keeper, or whatever she was.

"Shall I bring you a cup of tea, Madam? I have
very nice tea, and I can put a few drops of rum in, if
you desire."

"No, no rum!" I entreated as piteously as though
pleading for my life.

"Without rum, and very hot," ordered Pacheco.

The woman left the room. I closed my eyes again.
My brain felt like a hive of bees. Pacheco continued
to stroke my head, and his touch alleviated the pain.
I could feel him smoothing the pillow, and putting
back my hair, all as gently as a sea breeze playing
with my curls. Again I heard steps, and the clatter
of the woman's heels.

"The tea, sir. Will you give it to her, or shall I?"

"Bring it here, please."

I heard him stir the tea, then felt the spoon between my teeth. The effort of swallowing fatigued
me. After the first sip I shook my head. At the
second I sat up suddenly, and in doing so spilled the
contents of the cup over the vest and trousers of my
nurse. Then the audacious fellow, with unheard-of
familiarity, actually said,

"You don't want it now, love ?   Or shall I ask for another cup ? "

And I ?   Merciful heavens !   I am sure of this.   I answered him as affectionately, using the same tone of intimacy.

"Never mind, dear.   It is getting dark, and we must return to the city.   Let me see if I am able to rise.   What nausea !   Good heavens, what nausea ! "

I stretched out my arms confidently, and the wretch held me firmly while, hanging about his neck, I managed to slip to the floor.   With great care and politeness he helped me with the buttons.   He pulled out my draperies, handed me hat, pins, gloves, fan and umbrella.   I could scarcely see, but that I attributed to the darkness of the wretched little room.   But when aided by Pacheco I tottered across the threshold, I saw that night had closed in.   Way beyond the fence which enclosed the field I could make out the confused dark mass of the Fair, dotted with innumerable dancing lights.

The calm of night and the fresh air acted like a cold douche.   My head cleared.   The burning sun and the alcoholic spirits of that diabolical wine seemed to escape from my brain in bubbles, like foam from an open champagne bottle.   But in place of my active brain, there appeared to be nothing — an empty space, swept clear as with a broom.   I was idiotic, annihilated.

Pacheco guided me to where the carriage waited.

The lamps of the berlin flared at us from the entrance to the Alameda, just where we had ordered the coachman to wait in the morning. In silence we got in, and I sank almost senseless on the seat. Pacheco gave an order, and the carriage drove off.

Merciful powers! and I had thought myself free from the ship, the ocean swell, and all my maritime fancy! What a mistake! The real voyage was just beginning. We were in the cabin of a Transatlantic steamer which rolled every two minutes, or plunged down into ocean abysses, dragging me with it. Pacheco's voice was no human tone; it was the wind playing through the rigging.

" Are you angry with me, dear? " sighed the southwest wind. " Don't be angry. You know how reserved and prudent I was until you pressed my hand. Forgive me, dearest; it hurts me so to see you grieve. It is strange, but I feel almost frightened at the idea that you may be vexed at what I said. Poor child, you don't know how bewitching you looked, lying there. Your eyes flashed — what eyes! Come, lean on my shoulder. Rest, dear, and sleep."

These may not be his words, for the sound was nothing but a soft murmur in my ear. But one sentence I remember positively. Doubtless it was uttered between two waves.

"Do you know what they said at the house? That we must be newly-married people, ' for he treated her so lovingly, and could not do enough for her ' ! "

I can swear that I remember nothing more. Yes, very vaguely, that the carriage stopped, and Pacheco helped me mount the steps; that half fainting as I was, I retained enough instinct of caution to beg him not to come in. I don't know what he said at parting, but our farewell was brief and cold. Diabla nailed her eyes curiously on my face, as I explained that the sun had given me a bad headache, and that I would go straight to bed. It is clear that she can see through a mill-stone. She is no simpleton, and I wonder what she thinks of me at this moment.

I rushed into my room and threw myself on the bed, face to the wall. Soon I sank into a sort of stupid slumber, but by three in the morning the comedy recommenced, and I suffered it all over again. I didn't wish to call Diabla — to increase her suspicions. But what a night of horrors! What nausea, what nightmares! What fever and stupor, and what a headache this morning!

And worst of all, what a compromising adventure, what an alarming liaison, and, since there is no begging the question, what a dreadful fall!

CHAPTER VIII

ADMITTED ; but let us also admit that after behaving so correctly at first, Pacheco did ill to play me such a trick at the end. If circumstances, that is to say, the unexpected circumstances in which I found myself, gave him a certain encouragement, surely no real gentleman would have taken advantage of that accident. On the contrary, a man shows his breeding (if he has any) precisely at such junctures. I was completely upset, and the more helpless that never in my life had I been entangled in an affair of that kind. I was really irresponsible, what with the heat, the excitement, and the Manzanillo ; while he, the rascal, was, no doubt, as calm and collected as if he had been cooling at the bottom of a well. As I said before, he took an audacious, a nameless liberty.

The more I think of it ! Why, a man with whom I had not exchanged a dozen words twenty-four hours before ; who has never been inside my doors ! I can't help recalling a novel I used to read as a girl where the heroine finds herself in a position similar to mine, and torments herself by asking over and over, " Do I love him ? Do I love him ? " The little fool ! As if it were always a question of love. If I were to ask myself anything it would be, " Do

I know this gentleman?" For upon my word, I couldn't so much as tell his second family name! But one thing I do know — I detest that fellow, and I consider him a deliberate scoundrel! Haven't I good reason, and to spare? Let any woman put herself in my place.

And now — Suppose I refuse to see him, as I naturally should; give strict orders about him to the servants? He will be furious, of course, and boast of his conquest to the Duchess. Very likely he is one of those rakes who love to proclaim their victories from the housetops. I can imagine it. And still, allow him to present himself coolly here? No; that I cannot endure. In the first place, I should die of shame at the sight of him. Besides, in these affairs, if one does not begin with heroic measures there is no knowing — No; my first idea is more natural. I am not at home to Don Diego. Then he will write. I do not answer. Then after a few days, as I am about to leave Madrid — Yes; I shall have no further trouble.

But now, Asis, looking at the matter calmly, is Pacheco really the sole culprit? How about you? Come, be honest! Did any one force you to satisfy that wild caprice of visiting the Saint Isidro in company of a man you barely knew by sight? Or to breakfast with him in that vulgar booth, as if you were a sausage seller of the commonest type? Why did you drink that heady adulterated wine? Don't you know well enough that the sun affects your head, even if you drink nothing?

The truth is that after hearing what the Duchess said you were crazy to see the Fair for yourself. But you must remember that the Duchess is a privileged character. For certain persons the social regulations relax. The Duchess, moreover, is experienced, wide-awake and self-possessed. No man would dare take a liberty with her, unless she really wished it. And then, her rank makes people accept her charming eccentricities, while in other women they would reprobate the same actions as evincing shameless levity. Some persons may do anything, but you are not one of these. You are an ordinary society woman. You belong to the rank and file, and you must keep step. Undoubtedly Pacheco saw from the very first that you — No; it is not just to lay the whole blame on him.

After all, Pardo was right. We are all the same, true children of the people. Education polishes us thirty years running; then, all of a sudden, the original bark crops out, rough as the first day. In given cases the educated person acts precisely as the peasant would. In this instance I have acted like a shop-girl.

No, I acted like a fool. I was incredibly stupid. I didn't know enough to be on my guard, but I had no evil intentions. When all's said and done, the miserable fact remains, and weighs like lead on my conscience. This has never happened to me before, and never shall again. I am sure that I shall never commit the same folly twice. Now, to remedy the evil. Double lock the door; the cold shoulder; not a syllable! This young spark shall never see a hair of my head again. I take the train for Galicia, and soon, too. I declare the house in a state of siege; not a fly shall enter. He shall see whether it is easy to turn my head when I have my wits about me.

CHAPTER IX

MORE or less in this fashion would the lady have drawn up her confession had she confided to paper the thoughts which were surging through her brain. We do not guarantee her absolute sincerity, even in this dialogue with her own conscience. We dare not affirm that the Marchioness of Andrade omitted no detail which might aggravate her guilt, on the score of carelessness, levity or coquetry. Everything is possible, and one should use caution in vouching for one's nearest friend in this kind of confession, which is always made with halting tongue, and with mental reservations.

Still we cannot deny that she used great frankness in her account of the terrible episode, the more terrible to her because until that fatal hour she had walked with firm and happy step in the narrow path of virtue. Her good conduct in this respect was due rather to her disposition than to parental care, for her training had been neither rigid nor careful. Asis was an only child, motherless from an early age, and indulged in every caprice which a young heiress could invent in a small town like Vigo. By the time she had reached twenty she had been presented at the Casino balls, taken part in all the fairs and pilgrimages, and visited every one of the naval vessels which were constantly running out and in the Bay of Vigo. And withal, she had never been guilty of any impropriety. For who would be severe enough to term improper a correspondence with a certain fascinating lieutenant of the navy, whom she saw occasionally when the *Villa de Bilbao* was cruising in Galician waters? While this correspondence was still going on, Asis's father, a rich merchant, began to feel an itch for Government contracts, and the consequent necessity for going into politics. He persuaded an accommodating district to return him to the Cortes, and began to take Asis with him when he visited the capital for the session, or for the business connected with his contracts. On these occasions they enjoyed the hospitality of the Marquis of Andrade, a cousin of Asis's mother. Our heroine was the fruit of a marriage between ducats and blazon, a kind of alliance profitable to both parties, and so common in Galicia and everywhere else that aristocratic family portraits no longer make any wry faces, nor do the noble ancestors turn in their graves with disgust.

The Marquis himself was a Councillor of State, a widower without children. He still preserved a fringe of hair around his bald crown, and his manners were most agreeable. (At court there are no sour old men.) He was man of the world enough to understand how to insinuate himself, though a quintogenarian, into the affections of a young girl. Asis began to show him her lieutenant's letters, in fun; but she ended by writing to the lieutenant, in earnest, that everything was over between them. And so it proved, for no graceful shade in white cap and blue jacket with gold anchors ever appeared at the foot of the Marquis's nuptial couch.

The Marquis tactfully avoided any show of jealousy, and endeavored to make conjugal life pleasant to his young wife. He went so far as to separate from a sister, with whom he had lived since his first marriage, because her taste for seclusion and religious practices clashed with the natural gaiety of his youthful bride. He opened his purse freely for dressmakers and milliners, and cheerfully accompanied Asis to theatres, receptions and balls. His good sense kept him from any display of passionate ardor inappropriate to their combined ages. He left slumbering what it was foolish to awaken, and by this rational system he secured for himself seven years of tranquil happiness, and the additional blessing of a little daughter. It is true that the child seemed but a feeble blossom, which revived only in the bracing air of Galicia. A sudden illness cut short the existence of this model Councillor of State, and left Asis a rich young widow, well established in society and on the best of terms with her conscience.

She passed her winters in Madrid, where her daughter attended a fashionable French school as day pupil. Her summers were spent in Vigo with

her father.   Sometimes (as this very season) Asis
sent her daughter away with the grandfather, at the
close of the Cortes, for the benefit of the sea air.
She let the child leave her willingly enough.   Her
maternal love was what her conjugal love had been ;
a calm affection, free from the divine madness which
sets the soul on fire and gives a new meaning to
existence.   So the Marchioness of Andrade lived on
in placid comfort, proud of having shaken off her
provincial husk.   Well pleased, too, that she had
preserved her honor intact like the noble ladies of
Vigo, who never take a step but the whole neighborhood knows whether it was with the right foot or
with the left.   Her leisure moments were filled by
thinking, for instance, that her last dress was as
pretty as the one Worth had just sent the Duchess,
and far less expensive.   That she was in high favor
with Father Urdax, thanks to having joined a chari-
table society in good odor with the Jesuits.   That her
reputation was irreproachable, while her name figured
to advantage in the society columns ; showing the
possibility of serving Mammon without forsaking
God, since neither the world nor her Lord could
allege the slightest reason for turning the cold
shoulder on her.

And now !

CHAPTER X

HEARING the bell jingle once more, Angela hurried in to see what was wanted. She found her mistress sitting up in bed, leaning on her elbow.

"Whoever calls, I am out, you understand, no matter who it is!"

"Out to everybody. Yes, Madam."

"To every one, without exception. Don't forget it!"

"Certainly not, Madam; not even a cat shall come in."

"And draw my bath."

"The bath? But Madam is ill?"

"Not now," replied Asis shortly. ("What a mania these maids have for meddling.")

"And the orders for the carriage? Roque has been twice already to inquire."

At the coachman's name Asis felt a dreadful qualm, as if he represented society, duty and everything which she had trampled under foot the night before. The coachman, indeed! He must suspect —

"Tell him to — to come in a couple of hours, at quarter past four, or five, for a drive. No; say half past five."

She jumped out of bed and slipped on her dressing-gown and Chinese slippers. She felt low-spirited,

and ached in every limb ; still a certain feverish
excitement urged her to do something, walk or drive ;
get away from herself ; forget her own personality.

"What a life a woman must lead who is always
involved in these affairs," thought she.   "Certainly
the game is not worth the candle.   How I hate con-
cealments and contrivances.   It is plain enough that
I was born for a quiet, decent life.   I wonder if he
will have the audacity to attempt to see me again ? "

While waiting for the bath Asis scrupulously per-
formed all the little toilet operations which should
precede it.   She filed her nails, brushed her teeth,
cleansed her ears carefully with a tiny sponge and an
ivory scoop, and rubbed her neck with a horsehair
glove, covered with almond and honey paste.   With
each hygienic operation some part of her body regained its accustomed freshness, and little by little
she felt the brand of yesterday's levity disappear.
Confounding the physical with the moral, Asis almost
persuaded herself that she was regenerating as she
became clean.

When Diabla announced that the bath was ready
her mistress went into a small dark room lighted by
an oil-lamp, and plunged into a tub lined with porcelain, like an agate saucepan.   The luxurious bathing
appointments described in modern novels exist only
in palaces, never in rented apartments.   What a
sense of comfort !   The burning shame and lassitude
of the adventure would dissolve in the clear warm

water. Now they were written all over her body in the dust of that vile Fair. How thick it was, and how sticky! How pertinaciously it had worked its way through her stockings and underclothing! " Plenty of clean warm water," thought Asis. " Let me wash away the grossness, the barbarity ; wash away the audacity, the thoughtlessness ; all the — I need soap, too, and more and more ; then the cologne. Ah, how good that feels ! "

This half-delirious notion of washing away the stains on her honor with cologne and scented soap took such hold on Asis that she came near rubbing the very skin off in her energetic efforts. When the maid handed her the Turkish towels she continued her frictions, half moral, half hygienic, till she felt completely worn out. Then she let herself be robed in clean linen with the sigh of one who throws off an immense load of care.

The carriage arrived a short time after the conclusion of the toilet. Asis had selected the quiet dress of a lady who does not wish to attract attention. She had her hand on the door-knob, when Diabla suddenly inquired,

"Will Madam return for dinner ? "

"No," said Asis, and added in the explanatory tone of one who wishes to avoid evil constructions, "I shall dine with my Aunts de Cardeñosa."

When actually seated in the carriage she breathed freer. There was no longer the dread of seeing

Pacheco appear at the door.   But after all, how unlikely that he should have come !   Probably he would
never think of her again.   These lady-killers, as soon
as they can boast of a conquest, good-bye, sweetheart,
with them !

Well, all the better.   Would it not be unheard-of
luck to get out of a serious situation in that simple
fashion ?   And here Asis's voice took on a certain
sonority as she said to the coachman,

"Drive to the Castellana, and afterwards to my
aunts' house."

That proud intonation really meant, " You see,
Roque, we don't lose our heads every day in the
week.   From now on, I am back in my old rut."

The carriage rolled off, and presently took its place
in line on the Castellana.   There the press was so
great that at times it was impossible to advance or
recede.   In this forced standstill amusing scenes
would occur.   Ladies whose mutual acquaintance was
of the slightest would be obliged to remain face to
face for a certain time.   With no common subject of
conversation, they would sit there with the same
stereotyped smile on their lips, regarding each other
slyly, seeking occupation in the arrangement of some
trifle, and praying all the while for some movement
in the sea of vehicles which might bring the uncomfortable situation to an end.   Once or twice Asis found
herself at close quarters with an open hack, on the
back seat of which were crowded three roisterous

young fellows, Government clerks in all probability,
who kept up a running fire of foolish slangy compliments. She had just to bear it, without knowing
which would be more dignified, to smile openly, or to
look very serious and pretend to hear nothing. Nor
was it pleasant to have for close neighbor some
Englishman's spirited horse which thrust its foamy
bit in the window, and shook the froth all over the
bunch of white lilacs which, fastened into the card-
case, perfumed the whole carriage. These little incidents diverted the Marchioness of Andrade, and made
her enjoy all the more the repose and sweet calm
induced by the perfumed air, the quiet animation of
the drive and the comfortably cushioned carriage.
Suddenly she caught sight of a well-known face.
" Why, that is Casilda Sahagun perched up on the
coupé of her brake! Where can she have been?
Oh, yes, I remember. That private bull-fight by
Perico Gonzalvo's set."

Asis called to mind the organization of the amateur
taurian exhibition, and the pretty satin programmes.
How they had laughed to read, for instance : Bande-
rillos, Fernando Alfonso Hurtado de Mendoza as Pa-
jarillas. What fun they had had making up the
programme at the Duchess's house that night! And
Asis had been invited. What a shame to have forgotten it! The Duchess looked as charming as ever,
in a black mantilla and bunch of red pinks that made
her a Goya picture. The young fellows were all

wrapped up in their red and purple cloaks, models
of propriety and elegance. They had fought that
afternoon like heroes no doubt ; and now that the
sport had changed they were equally at home in
showing off their fine costumes to the admiration of
the whole Castellana, which had no eyes but for the
brake and its striking occupants.   Asis felt more at
ease after passing the Sahagun party. Her good
sense told her that no one of that gay group, continually occupied by some important event in the
political or social world, or by some striking scandal
in high life, would never dream of suspecting her
simple little adventure at the Saint Isidro.   Moreover, for the next few days nothing would be talked
of but the private bull-fight.

The conviction that her escapade was unlikely to
become public received further confirmation during
her visit with her aunts.   These ladies were a couple
of good, sad-eyed, flat-chested, antiquated spinsters,
timid, gentle, and, in spite of fifty years well told,
still unemancipated from the eternal infancy of
womanhood.   Their conversation turned chiefly on
devotional subjects, but they would occasionally discuss the family affairs of the Andrades, and other
distinguished families.   They had formulas for every
occasion in life.   At weddings they assumed an affectionate, inquiring air, as if they were inhaling the bouquet of the wine which had never passed their lips.
There were certain resigned shrugs, certain melancholy

archings of the eyebrows, certain phrases which they always used in cases of severe illness, at the death of old people, or when called on to comment on the wild oats sown by young men of good family. They were truly religious women, and, in consequence, never talked scandal, or passed uncharitable judgment on any human being. But for them life presented but one side, the obverse ; that is to say, the side which each one chose to show to the world. With, or in spite of all this, the two ladies were considered to belong to the best society, and their visiting-cards made a good show in any of those porcelain bowls in which social distinction is piled up in the form of pasteboard.

At first Asis found the stupid family dinner, and the anodynous evening which followed, soothing to her feelings. The last traces of headache and fever disappeared in the calm society of these excellent and respectable ladies, who treated her as they always had done; that is to say, with the greatest kindness. She realized that they would never suspect her of anything wrong.

As mind and body alike became tranquil she began to ask herself whether "that thing" were not some nightmare, some figment of imagination.

But as soon as this state of calm, so necessary to her nerves, had been attained, Asis began to feel horribly bored. She was getting sleepy, and longed for fresh air. She yawned in spite of heroic efforts,

and turned and twisted on her chair as if the soft
cushion were stuffed with pins, point up.   The
symptoms became so marked that the aunts could
not help noticing their niece's discomfort.   With the
greatest solicitude they began to offer her another
chair, a cushion at her back, a foot stool.

"Don't trouble yourselves.   I am very comfortable
— a thousand thanks."

Not daring to consult her watch, Asis stole a
glance at the mantel clock.   It was an Apollo of
gilded bronze, grasping his lyre with an air of great
determination.   In all the years the god had stood on
the chimney-piece, the good ladies had never noticed
his scanty drapery.   After the fashion of drawing-
room clocks, it had refused to go from the very first
day ; so that Asis obtained little consolation from
that quarter.   Do what she would, she could not
keep from yawning.   She fanned herself furiously,
and answered at random the questions about her
daughter's health and her own plans for the summer.
The hours dragged by, each drugging her with an
new opiate of dulness.   Every carriage-wheel in the
retired street startled her like an electric shock.   At
last a rumble of wheels ceased at the door.   Heaven
be praised !   Her animation came back as if by
magic.   When the servant entered to announce the
arrival, she had gathered heroism enough to feign
indifference, and actually said,

"Thanks !   Tell Roque to wait."

But a few minutes later, alleging early rising that morning, she took leave, printing a glacial kiss somewhere in the air near the parchment cheeks of her aunts, and hurried downstairs, repeating mechanically,

"Yes — some day very soon — I've had such a pleasant evening — to-morrow, certainly — What? Oh, yes, the circulars about the Orphan Asylum. Regards to Father Urdax."

As she rang her own door-bell Asis felt a curious presentiment. It is rather the fashion to laugh at presentiments, but they are very real nevertheless. Those who deny them are victims of what we may call myopia of the heart ; they are coarsely organized beings who will not admit that others may possess a delicacy of perception which Nature has denied to them. While the bell was vibrating Asis experienced a tingling in her veins and a tremor in all her limbs, as if through that simple action of ringing the bell she had come to a turning point in her life. And she felt no surprise, although indeed a spasm of emotion so violent that she almost fell to the ground, when the door was opened, not by Diabla, not by the servant, but by her new-made lover, Diego Pacheco.

CHAPTER XI

THE curious part of it was that, far from appearing surprised, Asis saluted her friend as if it were the most natural thing in the world to find him there at that hour of the night. And Pacheco, on his side, omitted no form of courtesy which a gentleman should use in meeting a lady whose position and character, if not her age, demand respect. He stepped aside to let her precede him into the little boudoir, where the great lamp with its rose-colored shade was burning dimly, and on entering, remained standing near the door, as if waiting to be dismissed.

" Sit down, please," stammered the Marchioness, still greatly upset.

He did not sit down, but approached her very slowly, as if lacking confidence in his reception. From his bearing you would have taken him for a man unused to society. But this diffident air (which Asis attributed to refined hypocrisy) contrasted charmingly with his graceful figure and the elegance of his attire. Pacheco indeed was an admirable example of the fine gentleman of modern Spanish society. Seeing him to all appearance so penitent, Asis recovered her presence of mind, and began to take

courage. "This is the opportunity to read my gentleman a lesson," thought she. "Is he really afraid?
Well, we shall soon ascertain."

The fact is that Asis in her inexperience had pic-
tured to herself Pacheco entering with the air of a
conquering hero, and opening the interview with a
brutal hug or similar demonstration. But now that
he seemed so subdued, heaven be thanked! she might
take the upper hand, and keep it. With this praise-
worthy intent Asis opened her lips, but it was only
to murmur unconnectedly,

"So you are here, it seems — I should like to —
that is to say, I — "

Pacheco was now very close to her as she stood
near the table. He looked at her narrowly, and then
began in a plaintive tone,

"Scold me all you wish, but don't say anything to
the servants. This is all my fault. It took me a
quarter of an hour to persuade your maid to let me
in. I paid her all manner of compliments, but nothing would do. You had given orders. So at last I
had to tell her that you — well, that you expected
me to-night and wished to keep every one else out,
so that we might be alone. You see I am to blame;
I deserve anything you can say."

He offered this astonishing explanation in a languid
voice, and with such a melancholy air that it was
difficult not to feel that he was the aggrieved party.
At first Asis stood petrified, but her tongue soon

loosened, and the words came bubbling out to relieve her conflicting emotions.

"Yes, indeed, I do think you deserve a good talking to, for compromising me with my own servants. That is why they hid and let you come to the door when I rang. Simpletons! Angela shall hear from me, I tell you. And as for Perfecto, I've a great mind to turn him out of the house this very night. Your own servants are your worst enemies. Just let them see whether they can play the same trick on me twice! Did any one ever hear of such conduct? You do everything for them, and then they turn about and sell you to the first stranger who talks them round."

Asis herself realized that this voluble scolding and wringing of hands was far from dignified. Moreover, it was like crying in the wilderness, since the kitchen lay too remote to permit the objects of her wrath to catch a single syllable. Nor did Pacheco seem alarmed at the warm reprimand; on the contrary, it actually appeared to raise his spirits, for he came still nearer, and stooping over the irritated lady began to stroke her temples very gently. She drew back, but not in time to prevent an arm from stealing round her waist, while a low voice murmured in her ear,

"Why are you so angry with the servants, dearest? Haven't I told you they were not to blame? That maid of yours is a perfect treasure. I offered her money; but no, she would be cut in pieces first.

She is so attached to you.   And she said at last that
if you would not be angry — If you call them now
it will make a scandal; and as for me, of course I
will go the minute you say so.   Of course I will go."

As he announced his readiness to go, Pacheco sat
down on the sofa, and gently pulled Asis to his side.
She began to be conscious of an agitation which did
not resemble the mock anger of a few minutes before.
After a little she said in a very low tone,

"Go, then.   For my sake, go at once."

"You won't spare me a minute, even?   Not one?
I feel so miserable.   If you only knew!   I couldn't
sleep; I didn't close my eyes all night."

Asis was about to ask why, but stopped herself in
time, realizing how absurd and inappropriate the
question would be.

"I felt that I must see you," went on the lover.   "I
wanted to know whether you were well again and
quite rested ; and whether you were still so much
vexed, or were beginning to feel a little indulgent.
Are you angry still?   And how is that poor head?
Let us see."

He pressed her head back on his shoulder, and
laid his hand on her forehead.   Asis endeavored to
resist, but felt her will power diminished by two senti-
ments; the first, a sort of pity, at seeing him so submissive, and the second, that eternal, that cursed
curiosity which ruined the first woman in Paradise,
which ruins all women, and perhaps the whole human

race as well! What is coming? What will Pacheco
say now? What will he do next?

For some little time Pacheco did not open his lips.
His delicate palm and thin, nervous fingers smoothed
Asis's temples gently, as if the fever of the preceding
day still continued and required the healing of that
simple caress. It seemed as if a magician's wand had
spread peaceful, loving silence over the whole room;
and the lamp-light filtering through the lace shade
illuminated the scene with poetic softness.

The room was furnished with the artistic pretension
which every living being in the society of to-day feels
called upon to exhibit, whether he knows anything
about art or not. The result was that pawn-shop air
which naturally comes from the conglomeration of
incongruous objects. Stools, low, coquettish arm-
chairs, little heart-shaped tables covered with plush,
S-chairs in which one could enjoy conversation and a
wry neck at the same time, lamps standing on slender
columns, plants in zinc jardinières, a porcelain dog
crouching as sentinel by the hearth — everything so
placed as to impede locomotion, and make the room
an archipelago, very dangerous to navigate without
preliminary chart studies.

And the walls? Not room for another nail! The
late Marquis, incapable of distinguishing a Titian from
a Ribera, had always shown himself a generous patron
of young artists of the fair sex. In consequence his
house was filled with water-color studies of street life.

Renaissance bullies and Louis XV ladies. There were studies so broad and free that the devil himself could not have told what they were meant to represent; tiny canvases of smoothest finish, framed in gilt five times the width of the picture; photographs with pompous and fulsome dedications. In a word, scraps of art which at least served to cover the commonplace wall-paper, and offer diversion to the eye. At that hour the sweet peace pervading the atmosphere, and the rosy light transmitted by the discreet lace, harmonized all these diverse objects and melted them into tender intimacy and silent complicity. Even the horrible Japanese mask, with a string of plush monkeys hanging out of one eye, softened its infernal grimace. The gay Manila shawl spread over the piano opened joyously its great flowers; the begonias near the half-open window trembled at the night breeze's caress. Only the porcelain bull-dog, posed like a sphinx, regarded the group on the sofa with alarming persistency. Dignified and energetic, he might have passed for a guardian stationed there by the ghost of the late Marquis. One might almost expect him to open his great jaws with a growl of defiance and prepare to spring on the intruder.

All this time Pacheco was talking very low to his lady love, with that tender, melancholy tone so characteristic of the Andalusian race.

"You knew what was coming yesterday, dearest? I swear you did, for women are very lynxes on those

points.   Ah! you are wise to keep silent, little witch!
You could see with half an eye that I was dead in
love — at first sight, too.   Only, you thought you
could make me keep my distance forever.   Talk about
knowing; why, you felt it by instinct from the moment
I threw away my cigar in the Park.   And you enjoyed seeing me suffer, naughty girl!   Take that for
your cruelty!   How charming you looked, you gypsy!
Did any one ever tell you that you were pretty?
Well, then, I tell you now, and I am worth half a
dozen.   Listen, dear; I had the words on my lips a
thousand times in the carriage.   I longed to call you
sweetheart, charmer, man-tamer — but, do you know,
I didn't have the courage.   If I had dared, I should
have smothered you with caresses and compliments — "

At this point Asis miraculously recovered her
powers of speech, and put in a word.

"No doubt — as you did to the waitress — and to
my maid — and — to any one who comes along.
Words never fail you."

Pacheco interrupted her with an energetic kiss.

"Don't make absurd comparisons, dear.   Those
silly things I say to pass the time and please the
women.   But with you, Holy Virgin!   That is something quite different.   I lose my wits completely
when I am with you.   This affection takes hold of
me in a most astonishing way.   I never before felt
out of spirits after an affair — like this.   Only now,

with you. Why I scarcely dare say anything to you.
I feel — well, half sorry, half proud, and upon my
word I almost wish we had returned to Madrid before breakfast. You don't believe me? By this I
swear!"

Pacheco made a cross with his fingers, and kissed
it devoutly after the popular Andalusian fashion.
Asis laughed against her will. Who could keep
angry with him? A laugh disarms the most furious.
"And now what shall I do?" thought she, summoning
all her presence of mind, all her feminine art. "Simple
enough, after all. Grant the rendezvous he begs for
to-morrow afternoon. Refusal would only stir him
to some mad act. Best to temporize, grant the request, and at the appointed hour be in any place
rather than where Pacheco waits. And now, to save
appearances, get him off as soon as possible. What
will the servants think? At this very moment, Diabla
is in the kitchen, and heaven knows what she is saying!"

CHAPTER XII

IT is painful to be obliged to recognize and record certain events ; but sincerity forbids that any essential point be omitted from this history. Our best resource is to adopt the indirect method, leaving the unfortunate circumstances to be inferred by the reader, who will thus be saved the shock of coming in direct contact with the insolent, shameless facts. By this means the novelist, as well, may skilfully disguise her natural disapprobation. Now as to the rendez-vous which the Marchioness of Andrade had accorded with the firm intention of absenting herself at the critical moment, the novel may keep discreetly silent. It will fulfil its high mission by giving a faithful account of what took place at the lady's door on the following afternoon — a simple scene, but highly significant to an observing mind.

The carriage had been waiting since five o'clock. At first the coachman had remained firmly seated on the box, with whip erect, blanket drawn correctly tight, and reins well in hand, heels touching, and hat gracefully raked. But after a quarter of an hour the quiet of the late afternoon and the tedium of waiting combined to drop mandragora on his eyelids. Soon his chin drooped, his hands relaxed, and from time to time a kind of whistling snore startled him back to consciousness. The horse, too, in the first moments of expectation, had stood proudly drawn up, ready to devour the distance to the Castellana. But when convinced that the séance promised to be lengthy, he settled heavily down, shook his bit, covering it with foam, blinked lazily and then decided to indulge himself in a light, short *siesta*. The very carriage had the air of resting heavily on its wheels.

The sun was slowly sinking in the west, its last rays mounting from story to story, kissing the window-panes good-night, and passing over to gild the tips of the acacia bower in the Recoletas, which was itself already enveloped in the blue haze of nightfall. The heat had become a trifle less intense. The lamp-lighters flitted about like glow-worms, and the streets began to show rows of glimmering lights. Carriage, horse and man slumbered on, resigned to their lot, without troubling to consider that for the dream journey no harness is needed; or to wonder if they would be more comfortable, the first in the carriage-house, the second munching his measure of grain, and the third at his favorite tavern, or cheering Guerrito at the afternoon bull-fight.

It must have been close on seven o'clock when a man emerged from the portal. He was young, of elegant figure, and walked fast, as if anxious to avoid the porter's recognition. He crossed the street and

paused on the opposite sidewalk to look up at the
windows of the Marchioness of Andrade.

No one there!

The man continued to walk on in the direction of
the Recoletas.

CHAPTER XIII

MAJOR PARDO was in the habit of passing the evening now and then with his friend and country-woman, the Marchioness of Andrade. On these occasions, they chatted gaily on a thousand topics, disputing, getting greatly excited, and enjoying immensely their tête-à-tête. Of courtship, properly speaking, not a word; although the world, that is to say, the Sahagun drawing-room, whispered that Don Gabriel had an eye on the property and agreeable person of the Marchioness. Other friends declared that Pardo was entirely disinterested, caring nothing for money, or for women either, since a grave disappointment he had suffered in Galicia. This gossip referred to a romantic and mysterious story about a niece of his — a young girl who, it was said, entered a convent in Santiago rather than be forced to marry Don Gabriel.

Whatever may have been his intentions, Pardo had decided to devote to his charming friend the evening of the very day on which the Marchioness's carriage had enjoyed the famous *siesta*. It was about nine when he rang the bell. Ordinarily the servants showed him in with the alacrity which proves that the visitor is a familiar and welcome guest. But that night Perfecto, the butler (whom Asis called Imperfecto, because of his propensity to do and say the wrong thing), exchanged perplexed glances with Diabla, and replied haltingly to the Major's questions.

"What is the matter? Is the Marchioness out? On Tuesday I know she usually — "

" Out ? N-o, not exactly ; that is, I mean — " stammered Imperfecto.

" No, Madam is at home," put in Diabla, seeing the embarrassment ; "but she is a little — "

" A little undisposed," declared Imperfecto, in a diplomatic tone.

"What did you say, indisposed?" cried the Major, raising his voice. " How long has she been ill, and what is the matter? Is she confined to bed?"

"No, sir, not to bed. Symbols of sick-headache, sir."

"I'm glad if that is all. I will leave a card and call to-morrow to inquire. Give the Marchioness my best compliments. Remember that!"

Just as the Major said this, Asis, in wrapper and slippers, appeared at the door of the reception-room.

"They always get my orders mixed up," cried she. "Of course I am at home to you, Pardo. Come in. What have general orders to do with intimate friends? Please come this way."

Don Gabriel followed her in. The little boudoir looked as charming, as fresh and inviting, as on the previous night. The lace shade transmitted the same dreamy, rose-tinted light. A bouquet of lilacs and white roses was withering on the mantel. As the Major took a seat in his favorite armchair, his foot struck something half hidden in the folds of the Turkish rug in front of the divan. He stooped mechanically and picked up a small object. Asis reached her hand out eagerly, and, absent-minded as Pardo really was, he could not help noticing her agitation. The object he had found was an English leather card-case, with a silver monogram of two letters. It evidently belonged to a man. By an instinct of discretion and respect Gabriel pretended to have no eyes, and handed over his prize without attempting to make out the initials.

"Your Diablas and Imperfectos have given me a great fright," said he, trying to swallow his surprise. "Are their wits at wool-gathering, or did you really give that order?"

"I will tell you. I did give the order, but of course it did not include you. You might know that, for I called you back." Asis's tone was as penitent as if she were excusing a grave fault. She was very much disturbed, but made a tremendous effort to conceal her agitation.

"And what is really the matter? A headache?"

"Yes, my head aches dreadfully," and she raised her hand to her forehead.

"Then if I stay and talk to you, you will have a

bad night. It is better to leave you in quiet. The headache will pass off with a good night's sleep."

"No, don't go. On the contrary — "

"What do you mean by 'on the contrary?' I beg you will explain that mysterious phrase," cried Pardo, seizing any pretext for a discussion, which would give Asis an opportunity to recover herself.

"I will explain. It means that you are to take me out for a little walk, so that I may get a breath of fresh air."

"We might go to the theatre. They say the Padron Municipal at the Lara is rather clever."

"The theatre? Lights, heat, a crowd! Do you wish to kill me? What I need is exercise. I can go just as I am, with a wrap and a veil. It won't take me a moment to change my shoes."

"Nothing would please me better," said Pardo.

Asis sighed with relief when they were fairly in the street, with their steps turned towards the Park.

Some parts of the Salamanca Quarter give one the grateful illusion of being in the country. The clumps of trees, the fresh, sweet air, and the open sky, which seems higher there than elsewhere in Madrid, all lend themselves to the fancy.

It was a superb night. Asis looked up at the stars, and for the sake of saying something she began to compare them to the jewels she had admired at the balls that winter.

"That string of four little stars looks like the

Marchioness of Riacheula's pin — four diamonds,
which it makes you wink to look at! That constella-
tion — look, over there — resembles the pendant
which Torres-Nobles brought his wife from Paris;
there's even the middle yellowish star to correspond
to the Brazilian brilliant in the pendant. The charming planet, yonder, away from the others — "

"That is Venus. Is it not highly symbolic that
Venus should be such an exquisite star?"

"Ah! Pardo, that is how you always mix up human
and divine."

"But this time you mixed the two up, when you
compared the lamps of heaven to the jewels of your
friends. What a beautiful sky we have here in
Madrid," he added, after a short pause. "In this
respect we must confess ourselves beaten, Asis. In
Galicia everything is fresher, lovelier — all but the
sky. At home we look at our feet, but here we must
look above our heads to find the greatest beauty."

They were silent a moment. In that azure canopy
dotted with diamonds Asis and the Major saw the same
thing — a leather card-case. And by some curious
instinct each knew what was in the other's thoughts.

At length they reached the end of the Prado,
which was entirely deserted at that hour, with all
the chairs collected and piled up together. They
listened to the monotonous murmur of the Cybele
Fountain, and saw at the end of the little garden the
elegant Italian silhouette of the Museum outlined

through the irregular mass of conifers. No one was to be seen on the Prado, and the Cortes Square, by the light of its gas-jets, looked just as solitary.

"Shall we climb up to the Carrera?" asked Pardo.

"No, no; every other step we should meet an acquaintance, and to-morrow — sh-sh-sh — some little gossip at Sahagun's, or elsewhere! Let us go down towards the Atocha."

"And why do you give so much importance to idle gossip? Cannot a lady take a breath of air in company of a respectable friend? How stupid social regulations are! I might call at your house and stay till midnight, and no one ever know or care, and yet for half an hour's walk in the street — gossip!"

"What a mania you have for attempting to stem the current! We can never turn the world upside down. Let it roll on. Everything has its because, and all these precautions have some good reason behind them. What a delightful breeze!"

"It makes your head feel better?"

"A little; the air revives me."

"Shall we sit down awhile? This spot looks so inviting."

In truth the place did look inviting, offering solitude and company at once. At that hour the wide stone seats at the entrance to the Museum look as lonely as the most formidable desert in Castile, in spite of the neighborhood of the busy Cortes Square. All the air was rich with the perfume of acacias. Never

were better time and place for the Major, if he wished
to impart any bold confidence to his friend. But he
had no such confidence on his lips, for after sitting
down they both remained silent. Asis was not only
silent, but absorbed and melancholy.

That kind of pause cannot continue between a man
and a woman alone together at that hour of the night,
without causing them both to feel a certain amount
of confusion, at once pleasing and embarrassing. The
Major wiped his glasses, a favorite movement with
him, replaced them on his nose, and resolved to take
a bold plunge; for he judged that the lady wished to
come to an explication.

"It is no use to talk headache to me, Paquita;
something has happened, something of importance to
you. Don't be afraid of me. Aren't we old friends?"

"But there is nothing at all. What an idea!"

"All the better. I am delighted to hear it," said
Don Gabriel, retreating discreetly. "But if you have
nothing to tell me, I have something to tell you —
something which really worries me."

"About your niece?" asked Asis with real curiosity, for several times in intimate conversation Don
Gabriel had slightly alluded to that mystery.

"Yes, or at least my part of that affair — what
concerns me might properly be related to you. Heaven
knows how the world comments on it." (Pardo raised
his hat, for his temples were moist with perspiration.)
"I believe they say the poor thing abhorred me, and

buried herself in a convent to escape my pursuit. False, every word! She never abhorred me. She would shortly have come to love me with her whole heart, but at that time she could not distinguish her real feelings. When she first met me she was already compromised with a man — whose station — no, not his station, but — a man who could never become her husband. When the unhappy child realized this, she believed that the world was at an end for her — that the convent was her only refuge. Ah! Paquita, if you knew what suffering — what a soul's tragedy! It is astonishing that after certain events one can take up life again as before; visit, go into society, play the fool here and there, look at other women, and like them, too. As I admire you, for instance. You won't mind my saying that; you know I am not a suitor; only a true friend. My bluntness will not surprise you, for you are used by this time to my fashion of speech."

While the Marchioness listened to him, another voice, in her own heart, began to plead.

"Confide in him," it said. "Tell him something. Outline your dilemma, at least. He is eccentric, unpractical at times, but loyal always. With him you run no risk, and what a relief to speak out to some one! Perhaps he may give you good advice. Go on, you fool; doesn't he confide in you? Besides, you can't imagine that he is deceived by your silence. Explain about the card-case, if nothing more!"

But in spite of the urgent little voice, Asis merely said.

" And so she was getting fond of you without knowing it ? That is odd. How do you explain it ? "

" Ah! Paquita, I have given up trying to explain anything. There is no explanation for the phenomena of the heart, and the more one tries to puzzle them out, the more perplexing they grow. In our human brothers and sisters we find such anomalies, such contradictions, and through them all a certain fatal logic. As for sexual sympathy, or love, or what you may please to call it, that is the passion in which we find the greatest extravagances of all. And then, to the caprices and aberrations of this organ, here, add the maze of false ideas with which society complicates these psychological problems. Society —"

" Still harping on my daughter ? " interrupted Asis, with a laugh. " You put every sort of burden on society ; its back must be nearly broken."

" But see here, my dear friend. Society alone is responsible for my tragedy. You ask how? By attributing an exaggerated importance to what is comparatively insignificant, according to the laws of nature ; by making an accessory pass for a matter of prime importance. By — well, I can't explain myself, for fear of scandalizing you ! "

" Pardo ! How you excite my curiosity. I am dying to know what you were going to say. One may explain anything — in a proper way. Do you take me for a prude, with an old friend like you ? "

"Very well, then, since you give me leave. Where was I? Do you remember?"

"You were saying that principal and accessory were — it must have been some terrible heresy to make you hesitate."

"Yes, it was. You shall judge for yourself. I call accessory what in such cases the world calls principal. You understand?"

Asis kept silent a few minutes, because a young man happened to be passing near them. He whistled a popular air, and eyed the suspicious group with stealthy curiosity. When he had turned the corner she said,

"Well, but suppose I am wrong in my idea of what you mean?"

"You are not afraid to hear me speak out, really?"

Truly, from a certain distance their conversation might have been taken for a lovers' dialogue. Perhaps the only barrier which prevented it from being one, or ever becoming one, was a short, narrow piece of English leather — Pacheco's card-case.

"No, you do not frighten me," replied Asis. "Let us talk like two real friends, frankly."

"What courage you show! Then acknowledge that you will have no right to quarrel with me, if my tongue should slip — I shall try, though. Now, by accessory, I understand — what you women judge irreparable. Must I put it plainer?"

"Goodness, no!" cried the lady. "But in that case, what in the world do you call principal?"

"Something much rarer, and in consequence far more valuable; a sincere affection between the two concerned. How does that strike you?"

"Your idea is very singular!" exclaimed the Marchioness, thoughtfully.

"Let me demonstrate my theory. Firstly, as the preachers say, imagine that instead of being here in the Prado we are in a wilderness, leagues from the smallest hamlet. I am a brute. I take advantage of the occasion, of my superior strength; I fail in the respect I owe you. Is there two minutes afterwards any bond between us which did not exist two minutes before? None. It is as if you were to stumble against something sharp, hurt yourself, manage to walk along, tread more carefully in future, and — think no more about it."

"Describing the affair as you do," said Asis, "I should just say that you were a disgusting, atrocious villain!"

"Certainly. But let me take another example, my secondly. Beforehand I must beg your pardon for a shocking supposition. I am not a brute. I use no force, nothing of the sort. I merely prepare the situation carefully; excite in you the germ of passion which exists in every human being. No violence, unless perhaps moral violence. I am skilful; I say the right word, and you — in a moment of weakness —"

It was fortunate that the veil of night was spread

thickly about, that the street-lamps gleamed so distantly. Otherwise the Marchioness's agitation would have betrayed her a second time.

"He knows; he must know," she thought, with terror. It was in a hoarse, supplicating voice that she interrupted him.

"Don Gabriel, how horrible!"

"Horrible? See the difference between you women and us men. This horror, Asis, does not appear horrible to the men in your intimate circle. Not to the Marquis of Huelva, that severe moralist; not to your frank, good-humored papa; not to me, nor to any of us. It is a social convention. No one wonders at it, or cares a straw about it. But let the woman be in question, and we raise a hubbub to frighten the fiends, and make one believe Madrid afire. An unfortunate woman makes a mistake, and if we get an inkling of it, quick we throw ourselves on her like a pack of wolves. She must marry her seducer, or be classed with fast women to the hour of her death, be her subsequent life pure as a nun's. We sentence her, and wash our hands of her concerns. Marriage, or a lost woman — a professional Traviata. Good logic that, isn't it? You, innocent child, victim of your youth and inexperience, of the tyranny of the passions, of Nature's promptings, go rot in a convent; nothing else remains for you. Friend Asis, what idiotic conventions are these!"

While the Major was speaking, fancy showed him,

in place of the sycamore trees of the Prado, other, darker foliage — oaks and chestnuts. The fragrance of the acacias came to him like the scent of the wild mint which grows by the brooks in the Valley of Ulloa. By another phenomenon of interior optics the woman by his side saw a tiny house on the banks of the Manzanares, a small mean room, a great bed, a cup of steaming tea upset —

"Idiotic conventions," continued Don Gabriel, without noticing his companion's strong emotion, "but we pay dear for them at times. When they overpower us it may happen that a woman of noble instincts judges herself soiled, criminated, infamous for life, in consequence of one moment's weakness. Then, if unable to marry the man to whom she believes herself eternally bound, she annihilates herself, buries herself alive, bids good-bye to happiness forever and ever ; becomes a nun without vocation, or a wife without affection. Here you see the inevitable result of certain social dogmas !"

And again, as he murmured these bitter words, the Major's inward vision showed him, in place of the graceful silhouette of the Museum, the green walls of the Santiago Convent, the black bars of tragic remembrance ; and behind those rust-consumed bars, a pallid face with dark eyes like those of that sister to whom he had given the purest and most profound love of his whole life.

CHAPTER XIV

"COME, Pardo, you are too dreadful! Do you want to establish the same moral standard for men as for women?"

"Paquita — let us drop those stereotypes." (Pardo often used this word to condemn commonplace phrases or ideas.) "Men and women are made of the same clay. It is most detestable hypocrisy to accuse and criminate you with such rigor for what is passed over lightly in us."

"And conscience, my dear friend — and God?" Asis spoke with an affectation of seriousness and solemnity under which she veiled an immense satisfaction. The Major's detestable sophisms began to appear most sensible and agreeable. So far can passion pervert the understanding!

"Conscience! God!" cried Pardo, imitating the Marchioness's tone. "That is another theme, but let us consider it also. Are we speaking of sinners who believe, of Roman, catholic, apostolic sinners?"

"Of course. Do you imagine every one is as heretical as yourself?"

"Well, then, if we are considering believers, I will say that the question of conscience is entirely independent of sex. You may call me a heretic, but I have not forgotten my catechism. I could still rattle off the ten commandments, which are certainly addressed to us as much as to you. I know, too, that your confessor absolves and pardons you just as he does us. All that the minister of God demands of the penitent is repentance, and determination to amend his ways. The world, severer than God, demands absolute perfection — all, or nothing."

"No, Pardo; the Father tightens the screws a bit for us. For you a lighter pressure suffices," said Asis, advancing poor reasons for the delight of hearing them refuted.

"It may be, but that is only a prudent precaution, to prevent us from being scared away from the confessional — if we enter it! But no priest would dare tell you seriously that there was a special sin for women. So the matter reduces itself to positive and exterior results; in a word, to the social criterion. If no one knows the secret, it is no worse for you than for a man. And as for us men, no one cares that!" Here the Major snapped his fingers vigorously, to express the slight importance of masculine transgression. After a moment's silence he continued, "But if you attack me on the other side — "

"The other side," stammered the Marchioness, who felt no disposition to attack him on any side at all.

"If you throw self-esteem and self-respect into the balance, what each human being owes to himself — "

"That is just the point ; what we owe to ourselves," faltered Asis, red as a poppy.

"Yes, I admit, on that score, the woman's fault is always greater than the man's.   But this is the result of a false social idea.   The woman believes herself lowered before her own conscience because from childhood she has been taught to consider that act as the most infamous and irreparable.   A woman enters that state of sin as the damned enter hell — never to come out.   But we men are taught just the contrary, We are informed that it is shameful in a man to have no adventures ; that it is humiliating to refuse them.   So that just what makes men very vain makes you very vile.   Hereditary emotional preoccupations, Spencer would call them.   There is a good mouthful for you."

"That is nothing ; your society is making me a blue-stocking.   Every day you split my ears with some of those big words."

"And I should tell you," continued Pardo, warming as he discoursed, "that what I call accessory in a temporary liaison becomes even more accessory, to my mind, in a case of real love, where the thoughts are as closely united as if cemented together.   What I call accessory is merely the complement of something else much greater, eternal, comprehending this outward sign and everything else in life.   I can't explain it as I wish, and you are laughing at me ; so I would better stop."

But Asis was listening, listening with all her soul,

thinking that her friend had never seemed so inspired as that night, that he had never spoken so wisely, so profoundly. The Major's theories had wounded her grounded convictions at first; but before long they began to enter into her very soul, like well-aimed arrows of flame, kindling a species of incendiary bonfire by whose destructive light she saw trembling an infinite number of principles, hitherto considered firm as the eternal rocks. It was like the operation of removing a decayed tooth from the jaw; at first she felt pain and terror at the cold instrument, and at the pull; but afterwards a grateful sense of relief at finding herself free from the dead substance. Anæsthesia of the conscience by chloroform of evil doctrines one might call the chirurgico-moral operation.

"This man is extravagant," thought the patient. "He is saying the most unheard-of things to me; but he is right on every point. Justice speaks from his mouth. Is one to think oneself a criminal for a few seconds' error? I can stop at any time, and take good care to avoid a relapse. Of course if one were to make a practice of — But no; even he does not condone that! His theory is that certain things which happen so — how shall I say? without premeditation or initiative on one side, are not to be considered as indelible stains. Even Father Urdax is less severe in these matters than the hypocritical world. O merciful God! Here I am, throwing the blame on society just as Pardo does himself."

Arrived at this point the Marchioness was troubled by a twitching between the eyebrows and then in the nasal membrane. "Aaaash!" She sneezed hard, and shivered at the same time.

"Heaven forgive me, you are catching cold!" cried Pardo. "You are not accustomed to these moonlight rambles. Come, let us walk."

"No, it is not the dew which has given me a cold, it was the sun which affected my head."

"The sun? When?"

"Yesterday, I mean day before yesterday, going to — to mass at Saint Pasqual's. You know I go regularly, headache or no headache."

"That may be, but take my advice. We must walk along now. If you should take a chill on top of your sun-bath! Or even one of our charming intermittent spring fevers —"

"I'm not afraid," replied the lady, wrapping her shawl about her.

"Shall we go home now?"

"Yes; we might walk slowly in that direction."

The Major did not continue his moral analysis during the walk home. When Imperfecto opened the house-door Asis invited her friend to come in and rest awhile. But the Major refused, alleging that he must look in at the Military Club, read the foreign papers, and meet a couple of friends later at Fornos. He wished the Marchioness a respectful good-night, and ran down the stairs in double-quick time. This impartial philosopher, this moral anarchist strode along at the same unusual pace, and it is clear enough that he was indulging in this or a similar soliloquy, which might properly be put in the mouth of any supporter of the "stereotypes" so heartily condemned by Don Gabriel Pardo de la Lage.

"The widow has taken me in, and I believed in her irreproachable character. A whited sepulchre like the rest! I did not see the initials on the card-case. It might be — But who? For really there is no morsel of gossip about her, nor does she seem to have any hangers-on. Well, such is life! Disappointment after disappointment! And to think that at times I have been very near saying something serious to her! At least this time I have not lost my seat. My horse has stumbled, but I have managed to hold him up. If all disappointments would come in such good season!"

He walked along without noticing the trees of the Retiro, which massed themselves in mysterious clumps at his right. Nor did he smell the acacias. In his nostrils was the breath of other vegetation than the trim, courtly plants of the public park; he scented the wild perfume of great unpruned chestnut-trees, which bear the brown shining nuts they roast in November in the Valley of Los Pazos.

CHAPTER XV

Asis devoted the afternoon of the following day to making calls, a mechanical, fatiguing task, and one of the most irritating duties of the social compact. It is rare to find any one who submits to it without protesting inwardly or outwardly against the world and its tyrannies. It is not so bad, however, with houses such as the Sahaguns and the Torres-Nobles, where the visit begins and ends with the porter. At these aristocratic residences Asis held her card ready, with the corner turned down. At the sound of approaching wheels the porter appeared in the archway ready to receive the bit of pasteboard, with the usual question trembling on his lips,

"What address shall I give to Madam's coachman?"

The Torres-Nobles and other families of her acquaintance maintained the comfortable custom of never receiving except on certain regular evenings, so the formality of leaving a card was easily accomplished at any odd moment. But if a few in our heroine's circle lived on such a grand scale, many others were of less pretensions, and some friends or connections from Vigo were almost plebeian in the modesty of their surroundings. When visiting her country connections, Asis was obliged to enter narrow doorways and parley with the surly concierges. Worst of all, she was almost sure to obtain the disheartening reply,

"Yes, Madam, I believe she has not been out of the house all day."

Then would come three long, dark flights of winding stairs, redolent with odors from the various kitchens; the clumsy maid at the door, the boisterous reception and the same tiresome questions. She would sit a long half hour, with the untidy children swarming over her, listening to interminable details of family illnesses and Vigo gossip, distorted by the glass of distance. Truly it was detestable, and Asis detested it cordially. Nevertheless she consulted her list this morning, and said to herself with a profound sigh,

"There is Pardina's widow, and Doctor Cela's mother, and, above all, Rita. I must go to her because the baby has been so ill with diphtheria; and then she is Pardo's sister!"

Although the round of visits proved singularly tiresome, especially as most of the ladies were at home, and the conversation would have bored a plaster statue, Asis turned homeward with a greatly lightened spirit. The devotee stills his pricking conscience by reciting a dozen rosaries, with Our Fathers *ad libitum*. In the same spirit, Asis, who felt herself a social infringer, or at least on the brink of becoming one, gave up her day to minute fulfilment of social law; and as the atonement induced such weariness of spirit, she was inclined to feel her sin half pardoned. And for that matter, she felt more determined than ever to put an end to her present irregular conduct. The Major was entirely right. Her fault in itself was comparatively unimportant; but suppose it should become public? Ah, then! To prevent scandal and further weakness, to guarantee the future — that was the real problem. She must cut down to the root. (Asis was personifying Virtue as an enormous pair of pruning shears.) And she could do it easily enough, for in sober truth her heart was not engaged.

"Let me see," thought the Marchioness, pursuing this last idea; "if some one should tell me that Diego Pacheco had gone home, that he was engaged to a charming girl, it would mean nothing to me. It would not cost me a tear. I might even feel thankful for release from a dangerous position. My course is clear. Why should he go? I am the one in danger. It is I who should take flight. I am to leave Madrid very soon in any case. This will be anticipating the journey by a few days only. What a relief to take the train for Galicia! To put an end to this constant dread, this trembling, when Diabla asks me the simplest question. How foolish I am, after all, to blush and stammer like a schoolgirl. Am I not a widow? Thank heaven, I owe no man an account of my actions!"

Still pursuing this train of thought she reached her own door, and started up the staircase. The lamp was unlit, as often happened on warm summer evenings. At the second landing, heaven preserve us! a man's figure came out of the shadow. Pacheco!

She repressed a scream as he caught both her hands violently.

"How is my darling? This is the third time I have called to-day, and they insisted every time that you were not at home. I could swear you had not gone out the first time. If you really don't want to see me, say so, and I won't trouble you. I will look at you in the street and in the theatre. But don't dismiss me through a jade of a servant, who laughs in her sleeve as she shuts the door in my face."

"No," stammered the Marchioness, "but you see I —"

"Then, dearest, you didn't mean to include me in your order?"

"No, indeed, not you," said Asis hastily, and with a tone of conviction. So spontaneous and inevitable is self-deception in certain cases.

"Then I may come to-night at nine?" asked Pacheco with sudden cheerfulness.

She made an expressive gesture of dissent.

"Don't you want me, dear? Perhaps you have some other engagement. Tell me the truth. I will be off like a damned spirit if you don't want me. I never have the heart to insist when I see I am not welcome. You shall never suffer a minute's embarrassment on my account."

Asis hesitated. Strange fact, and yet explicable by the illogicality which the difficult position of woman imposes on feminine conduct. What decided her assent was precisely the resolution of flight which she had just adopted in the carriage.

"Very well," she said at last. "Come at nine" (here Pacheco drew her close to him); "but — you will go at ten?"

"At ten! I might as well not come at all. I see, you really have something else to-night. Why don't you tell me so frankly?"

"No, I have no engagement, but — you know the servants — I don't wish to make a spectacle of myself before them."

Pacheco laughed.

"Never mind them. The man is an imbecile. Your maid is more wideawake, but you can send her out on an errand. Good-bye till nine, sweetheart."

And he hid his face in the Marchioness's hair, disarranging it sadly, and pushing her jaunty hat askew. She put her head-gear to rights as well as she could, and rang with a trembling hand.

Once within, Asis became greatly preoccupied. She took off her things in an absent way, leaving her gloves here and her hat there. Diabla gathered up everything, and returned each article to its proper place, not without a minute inspection, which Asis found importunate. Why had she not firmly refused the dangerous rendezvous? Of course, it would have been far better. And yet, for the few days that remained — Struck with a sudden remembrance she turned to Diabla.

"To-morrow you must look at the big trunk. I believe the hinges are loose. And call at Madam Armandina's to see about my hats. If they are not finished, tell her to hurry. I wish to get away as soon as possible."

"Madam is going to Vigo?" put in Diabla with hypocritical suavity.

"Of course. Go to the shoemaker's too, and to Angel Square, to see if they have mended my fan yet."

Giving these practical orders calmed her. No, she could not well have refused. And if she had, he would have been back in the morning. Dissimulation, compromise, these were her sheet-anchors until she was fairly out of Madrid.

She ate little dinner, feeling that peculiar constriction in the throat which always accompanies great anxiety of mind. She looked continually at the clock, but it was barely eight when she rose from the table.

"Angela" (her mouth felt so dry that she could scarcely articulate), "do you wish to take this evening to visit your sister who married the city-guardsman?"

"Oh! yes, Madam, but it is so far. The barracks are in the Panuelas, and it would take me the whole evening to go there and return."

"That does not matter. I will pay your car-fare, or take a cab if you like. The concierge will let you in, even if it is after midnight when you return. Hurry through your dinner, and you will have plenty of time. And by the way, hasn't your sister a little girl about six?"

"Eight, Madam, and a baby thirteen months old, who is teething, poor little dear."

"Well, you may take those things of Marujita's which I laid by the other day. They will do to make over for the little girl."

"Heaven bless you, Madam! Shall I take the castor hat with the white feather, too?"

"Yes, you may take it. Hurry now."

The hat with the white feather produced an excellent effect. For several days past the Marchioness had fancied that her maid cast disrespectful glances at her, and spoke in a tone of veiled irony. But after this splendid gift nothing could be read in Diabla's eyes but jubilant gratitude. She finished her dinner in five minutes, and very shortly presented herself before her mistress, in Sunday array, with frizzled bang and creaking new boots.

Asis tried to speak in her usual voice.

"Hurry, child; it must be late — quarter of nine at least."

"No, Madam, only twenty-five minutes past eight by the dining-room clock. Is there anything Madam wants before I go?"

"Nothing. Have a good time. How elegant you look! Will there be company at your sister's? Young men?"

Diabla simpered.

"Maybe, Madam. There is a young soldier from our province who is sometimes there. He is tall, with a black moustache."

"Very well, you may go now. I want nothing more."

What a provoking creature that Diabla was! Fifteen minutes after receiving her dismissal, she was still lingering in the kitchen. With ear glued to the door of her boudoir, Asis listened for the departure, biting her lips with nervous impatience. At last steps were heard, the creaking of new boots, a loud laugh from the kitchen, and the parting benediction, "Have a good time and spend little." The front door opened, then closed with a bang. At last! Heaven be praised!

As soon as the exasperating Diabla was fairly gone a religious silence seemed to descend on the whole place. Even the boudoir lamps shone with a light softer and more peaceful, if possible, than other nights. It was a quarter to nine. Pacheco would not arrive for twenty minutes or so. At last a gentle ring was heard, as timid as if the bell itself feared to commit the sin of indiscretion.

CHAPTER XVI

It was Pacheco, muffled to the eyes in a great red cloak too heavy for the season. He paused irresolutely in the doorway, and Asis was obliged to encourage him to enter.

"Pray come in."

Upon that the gallant unmuffled himself quickly, and inquired for the Marchioness's health.

During the first moments they always spoke thus, clinging to the social formulas, and talking of trivial matters only. Their greeting was a simple handshake. They would have been puzzled themselves to account for this strange lack of demonstration, which no doubt arose from the newness and unexpectedness of their relations. But this night Pacheco's quick eye noted a different element in his lady's reserve. He seated himself on the divan beside her, and after a very embarrassing pause said in a low voice,

"How coldly you receive me. Have I displeased you?"

"Of course not. What do you mean?"

"Oh! dearest, don't try to blind me. I know women like a book. I have put you out in some way. You wanted to do something else this evening."

" No, indeed ; I had nothing in the world to do,"
declared Asis warmly.

" Well, now, I believe it, for you said that as if you
meant it. But anyway you are not glad to see me.
When I spoke to you to-day you wished me a hundred miles off."

As he said this Pacheco began to run his long fingers with their beautiful nails through her hair, and
seemed to take delight in disordering the simple coif-
fure which Asis had arranged with so much care, after
the fashion of Madam Pioñgrande's.

" If I do not wish to receive you," said Asis, " I
have only to say so."

" Of course, dear ; that is as it should be. One
should be entirely frank. But you know sometimes
one feels obliged to feign a certain degree of affection,
out of compassion, or I don't know what. I've done
it scores of times with my sweethearts. Tired to
death of them, and trying to pretend just the opposite. For after all, it is pretty hard to say plainly to
any man or woman, ' I am tired of you ; all the illusion is gone.' "

" Who knows whether you are not passing through
that agony on my account ? " cried Asis archly, with
a charming air of mock modesty.

The young man made no other answer than a sudden passionate embrace, and a " Would to heaven I
were ! " which seemed to come from his very soul.
His voice had become so hoarse and dramatic that the

Marchioness felt a singular thrill run over her, as if she had received an electric shock.

"Why do you say, 'Would to heaven'?" asked she, imitating his tone.

"Because this is something so different, something I never felt before for any woman. From the first moment you made me drink a love-potion, you charming witch! Because I am intoxicated, mad with love of you, sweetheart, do you understand? Because you will be my ruin, as sure as God is in his heaven. My treasure, what magic is in your eyes, in your mouth, in every inch of your body to drive me into this frenzy? Come here and tell me, my joy, my despair, my adoration!"

The Marchioness was silent with astonishment, not knowing how to answer these impassioned utterances. But a sudden tumult of sound came to help her out of the embarrassment — that musical horror known as a street band.

"Listen to that," cried Pacheco, springing up and throwing open the casement.

"Are the neighbors giving us a charivari already? The poor devils play horribly out of tune. Come here and listen; it will split your ears."

With his Southern nature nothing could be more natural than this sudden transition from the most passionate sentiment to vivid interest in a common street incident. To take color from every passing impression is the very essence of an Andalusian's being.

"Come," he insisted; "here is a chair for you. Let us enjoy ourselves. In whose honor is this serenade given?"

"It is for the new grocery opposite," answered Asis, happening to remember some of Diabla's gossip. "On the other side, a few houses down the street. There, that is the door. We are in for a concert, I'm afraid."

Pacheco pulled an armchair towards the window and sat down.

"You uncivil fellow," continued Asis, laughing. "Didn't you just say that chair was for me?"

"It is for you," replied the lover, clasping her round the waist, and obliging her to sit in his lap. She resisted a little, but finally gave in. Pacheco rocked her as if she were a child, and petted her in the same protecting fashion. Her position forced Asis to put one arm round his neck, and after the first few moments she laid her head on his shoulder. The breeze floated lazily in the open window, bringing with it the faint perfume of acacias, and the combined odor of smoke and heated tiles, peculiar to Madrid in the summer season. It essayed in vain to move the curtains, but from time to time wafted in echoes of music, tolerable, thanks to distance and the night — that medium which softens and harmonizes the most discordant sounds. The proximity of the two bodies brought nearer the two spirits, and for the first time in that singular love adventure Pacheco and

Asis engaged in an intimate and affectionate conversation.

Their talk did not run on love. It turned on subjects which would seem insignificant written down, which are seldom discussed in real life, except in such moments of unpremeditated confidence. Asis multiplied her questions, insisting on minute biographical details. What was Pacheco's profession? What were his hobbies, his tastes? What about his home life, his family, his intimate friends? Above all, Asis was anxious to know his exact age to the very month and day.

"Then I am older than you," said she, in a melancholy voice, when Pacheco had satisfied this last demand.

"I don't believe it," said the lover, "or at least it is only a year, or six months, perhaps."

"No, two years, certainly two."

"By the calendar, maybe, but you know, dear, the man is always the older because men live, and women merely vegetate. And for my part, I have lived for a dozen men. You couldn't mention a kind of deviltry I haven't dabbled in. I am passed master in the art of being a scapegrace these many years. If you only knew some of my pranks."

Asis felt a pang of curiosity mixed with an annoyance which she could not satisfactorily explain.

"Am I to understand, my good friend, that you are abandoned to every vice?"

"Abandoned? No, by all the saints, sweetheart.

It is a fact that I have made love to three hundred thousand women, more or less, but I truly believe that I never loved one of them.   I have committed every folly under the sun, but I have no real vices.   You wonder at this miracle ?   The truth is, that vices do not take root in me ; I am not naturally vicious, and, what is more, I should become a regular saint if I did not look out.   It is simply a question of the direction in which I am drawn.   Place me in conditions favorable to becoming a scapegrace, and I do as the others do.   If it's my cue to be good, no one gets ahead of me in that line.   So if I have happened to fall in with worthless society, what can you expect ? "

" Even in questions of honor you would float with the tide ? " asked Asis, rather alarmed.

Pacheco drew back as if a snake had bitten him.

" What a question you ask !   Do you take me for a vulgar seducer of youth ?   I make love to no women but of your type.   For the rest, you know that in Andalusia duels are not accounted crimes.   I have pinked one unfortunate fellow, and I wish I had never touched him with a ten-foot pole.   But who cares for such trifles ?   And outside of these, the devil has no hold on me.   I have gambled, winning and losing small fortunes.   I have tossed off my wine with the next, and as for affairs of the heart — it would be bad taste to speak of them to you.   Reward my discretion with a kiss."

" No, indeed ; I see you are a good-for-nothing

fellow!" cried Asis, turning away instead of comply-
ing with his request.

"You can't judge, dear. What I tell you is Gospel truth. I should like to know why God gave me
the breath of life! I am not only a harum-scarum
fellow, but also an idle dog, a drone in the hive. I
do nothing useful, and, what is more, I do not desire
to do anything useful. Why should I? My father,
dear old man, is determined to see me shine, serve
my country in the political field, enter the Cortes.
Bah! I see myself in the Cortes! Not one, nor
twenty such farces of patriotic activity would impose
on me. I should be bored to death there. But I am
not stupid or incapable either. I can always attain to
what I really set my heart on. But to tell the plain
truth, I have never exerted myself seriously in my
whole life, except in the conquest of some charming
woman. You doubt my ability to do anything else?
Little sceptic! Just show me something worth while.
The game which most people lose their sleep chasing
doesn't seem to me worth the powder. But to gain
a woman like you!"

Then very low in her ear, pressing her still closer
to him,

"This is the one thing which tastes sweet in this
bitter world, darling; to hold the woman you adore
close. To take her into your very heart. All the
rest is dust and ashes."

"But what you are saying is atrocious," protested

Asis, with great severity, for her Cantabrian puritan-
ism was aroused. "Are you not ashamed of being a
useless fellow, a coxcomb, a mere cypher at the left
of the figures?"

"What matter to you if I am, light of my eyes?
Can I be useless so long as I love you? Have you
vowed to love no man who hasn't his finger in the
political pie, and his faith pinned to some minister's
coat tail? But never mind. If you want me to become a political light, just say the word, and as sure
as my name's Diego you shall have your will. I will
leave to my grateful country a memory of glorious
days! Isn't that the way they put it? You don't
half know my talents. Tell me to become a second
Castelar, or a Canovas del Castilla, and it's done at
the word. Do you believe any of the political charla-
tans are worth more than this child? The only difference is that they sail with everything set, and I
scud along close reefed, just out of modesty, you
know, to let them keep the lead."

There was nothing for it but to laugh at the absurdities of that weathercock. Asis did laugh, and at the
same time she coughed a little.

" Good heavens! You are catching cold already!"
cried Pacheco with great concern. "Do put something on your head. You are so imprudent to sit out
here without even a veil."

"But I never wear anything on my head in summer. I am not delicate."

"To-night, at least, you must wear something, because I insist on it. If you were to fall sick, I should simply blow my brains out!"

Stifling a laugh, Asis sprang out of her lover's arms. In her haste she lost one Chinese slipper, which Pacheco picked up and replaced on her little foot with a thousand extravagant words of flattery. She hurried into her chamber and plunged into the great wardrobe in search of a little lace bonnet, mentally praying all the time that she might keep her head throughout this new trial. Her back was still turned to the faint light which came from the boudoir, when suddenly she felt two arms encircle her. A shower of ardent caresses followed close on this bold demonstration, and a deep voice repeated again and again in a really tragic accent,

"I adore you! My love chokes me! It kills me!"

It sounded like the voice of another man, vibrating with the profound tremor which violent emotion gives to human utterance. Asis was touched to the soul. She threw down the bonnet and stammered out, "Diego!" calling him for the first time by his Christian name.

"Why don't you say 'My own Diego, dearest Diego'?" cried he passionately, straining her closer in his arms.

"I don't know. Talking that way always reminds me of the stage. It seems artificial."

"I believe you. How you said it! 'My own

Diego!'" burst out the lover, imitating her tone. Then releasing her almost as suddenly and violently as he had seized her, he went on,

"Iceberg! What women they breed in your corner of Spain! I renounce them all. Sweep them off with the other rubbish to the dump!"

"One thing is certain," cried Asis with a burst of laughter; "that you are a rare combination of actor and lunatic! Who could keep a straight face in your company? Let me see. Here is a young man who has had four hundred sweethearts and a couple of thousand serious love-affairs. And now he is on his knees to me, like Petrarch before his lady Laura. In love with me, just everyday me! Exclusive privilege! Royal patent!"

"Take it in jest if you will, but it is the naked truth. Hundreds of fancies have caught my imagination, but never one like this. I swear it by these." And Pacheco made rapid crosses with his fingers. Then he continued as earnestly,

"My old charmers, my hottest flames, might pass me on the street by scores, and I should never recognize them; but you — why, if I were a painter I could draw your profile in the dark, so deeply is it stamped on my heart. Fifty years from now, when you would be getting to be an old woman, I could pick you out amongst a thousand other old women. My other adventures were vanity, caprice, mere sensuality, obstinacy — devices to kill time. But there remained one chamber of my heart empty, and I kept the golden key for you, you black-eyed gypsy! Do you doubt it? See for yourself!"

He drew the Marchioness towards the boudoir, threw himself back on the divan, then placed her hand flat on the left side of his vest. She felt a slight regular movement like the pendulum of a clock. Pacheco kept his eyes closed.

"I am thinking of other women, dearest. Be still and observe carefully."

"Your heart beats very gently," said Asis.

"Keep your hand there awhile — I am thinking of my last sweetheart, a blonde with the finest figure you ever saw. Do you see how still the little bird keeps? Now say something affectionate to me, if you can! Even if you don't mean it."

Asis searched for some term of endearment, and tried to give her voice the proper inflection. At last she uttered the commonplace "My dear!"

And lo! under her palm, like some gay spirit obeying a magician's wand, Pacheco's heart broke into the most agitated dance possible for that great muscle. It seemed like a frightened bird flapping its wings against the bars of its cage. Pacheco half opened his blue eyes. His sunburnt skin had paled a little. He rose with great precipitation, and walked out on the balcony, leaning against the rail as if to drink in the fresh air, and recover from a physical and mental shock. His attitude and expression made

Asis uneasy. She followed him, and touched him on the arm.

"Now you see what a fool I am," he murmured, turning half round.

"Do you feel ill?"

He turned again from the balcony, and threw himself down on a hassock in the boudoir. His persuasive eyes begged Asis to seat herself near him in the easy chair. When she had complied with the mute request, Pacheco bowed his head on her lap.

"Just see the effect of those two little words of love," he said, "the first I ever heard from you. Don't laugh, dear, for in my state of mind I might say something unpleasant. Since I lost my heart to you I have lost my good temper also. Don't say anything. Let your boy sleep."

That night Pacheco crossed the threshold before midnight struck, and before Diabla's return. When he turned to take his hitherto fruitless look at his lady's balcony, he was able to distinguish a white object in the dusk.

The Marchioness was exposing her burning cheeks to the cool night air. The intoxication of her senses and the paralysis of will power began to dissipate once more. A shipwrecked sailor cast on the shore feels with delight the belt of gold which he had taken the precaution to strap on before the plunge; and so Asis rejoiced, in the returning light of reason, that she had retained the spark of sense necessary to make her turn a deaf ear to a certain mad request.

"That would have been a fine affair! To-morrow the neighbors, the servants, the watchman, all the world and his wife would have known! Ah, me; I still feel the intoxication of that fatal Fair, and now I know that no medicine will cure me. Intoxication, sun-fever? Pretexts and nonsense! The plain truth is that I love him, and my infatuation grows stronger every day. His flattering tongue turns my head. He pretends that I have given him a love-potion, but it is I who have tasted it. And there is no remedy. I can't wrench myself free. When he leaves me I see my criminal folly plain as day; but as soon as he returns again it is all over with me. I know that I am lost."

Here she began to recall a thousand details which made up the beautiful mosaic of her lover's qualities and graces. His passionate wooing, his graceful manner of asking a favor; his personal elegance and distinguished bearing, as far from coxcombry as from provincialism; the rare mixture of popular spontaneity and high-bred courtesy; his flashes of wit, and a certain romantic melancholy — that union of extremes which is the charm of the characteristic Andalusian songs. All these were strong points to excuse her weakness, and account for the tyrannical affection which she felt creeping into her very soul. But at the same time she remembered other things, and chid herself severely.

"This must be the last time. There is nothing really good or superior in him. He is a lounger, a good-for-nothing, a vagabond almost. All that about my being the only woman — It is a trap, the habit of deceiving, a scapegrace's folly. As soon as he turns the corner" (Pacheco had accomplished this feat a few minutes previously), "he forgets what he swore five minutes before. These Andalusians are all born actors. Come, Asis, be sensible, be prudent. For this intermittent fever, my good girl, take railway pills, and extract of the Bay of Vigo night and morning, for four months. Bay of Vigo, when shall I see you?"

But the night breeze, making sport of the good lady's distress, whispered delicately in her ear,

"Light of my eyes, my pearl of sweethearts!"

CHAPTER XVII

THE Marchioness of Andrade and her maid were very busy overhauling trunks, valises and bags, a most necessary operation when you are about to undertake a journey. But what a distracting business it is. At the last moment the keys, for instance, are sure to be missing. It is no use to put them carefully away, saying, "Here is the key. I mustn't forget where it is. I will tie on a bit of red worsted to help me remember." The critical moment arrives. You search and search, turn the house upside down. Nothing! After a world of trouble, there's no help for it but send for the grimy, evil-smelling smith to make a new key!

Asis felt so nervous and out of temper that she showered on Angela these and similar complaints. The details of packing put the Marchioness in a very bad humor. It was so fatiguing; there was such confusion and noise. And then what to take, and what to leave behind! Heavy clothing seemed absurd, with the dog-days at hand; but who would trust the climate of Galicia, rainy, damp, and so changeable that six or more extremes of temperature often crowd into the twenty-four hours? Are you to leave your warm clothing here to laugh at you from the depths

of the dark wardrobe, while down in Vigo you freeze
to death, or wrap up in old country shawls that make
you look like a grandmother? Then, what with the
festivals and the Pastora balls, full dress was indispen-
sable. Country people are so odd. If they should
see the Marchioness of Andrade attend a ball in a
plain silk, they would lay it to pride, and say she
thought anything good enough for Vigo!

Certainly the last hours are enough to drive you
mad! Why had Angela forgotten to call for the
straw hats? And the mackintosh, still with those
hard buttons which catch on everything! And where
was the camphor for the furs, and the pepper for
the parlor carpet?

Diabla flew about in every direction, much abashed,
and did her best to reply to the shower of questions
and rebukes. After the first flurry, the sharp girl
found a skilful back-handed retort for her mistress.
If the preparations were behindhand, it was because
the Marchioness had decided so suddenly to go off a
month earlier than usual. Diabla's own summer
dress and other little trifles were not ready, for was
she not reckoning on the middle of June, about
Saint Anthony's Day? What reason had she to
imagine they were to go so early this year?

The Marchioness replied only by a repressed sigh,
and for two whole minutes she remained silent.
Then redoubling her grumbling, she went from wardrobe to bedroom. from attic to boudoir. and even

into the kitchen to scold Imperfecto for bringing
the wrong kind of tissue-paper, twine, pins and cotton-wool. With his stupid face and mouth wide open,
Imperfecto ran up and down stairs dozens of times in
the vain attempt to satisfy his mistress. The pins
were too large; he must change them for smaller
ones. She had told him gray cotton-wool, not
white; it was for packing. Of course the cheapest
kind would do! In one of these crises, Asis happened
to be crossing the hall just as the door-bell rang.
Contrary to custom, she opened the door herself,
moved by a sudden impulse, and found herself face to
face with her Diego.

Her first feeling was of annoyance, and very
slightly veiled. Who would have looked for Pacheco
at that hour, half past ten in the morning? Not that
Asis looked like a slattern, in torn gown and slippers
down at the heel; for her pride would have forbidden
that, even on a desert island. But her white China-
silk wrapper showed festoons of cobwebs, and even
some smutches of dust, the result of her encounter
with the dirty trunks. Her hair, too, was coiled up
carelessly, with loose ends protruding here and there.
The dust had settled in a thin layer on her face, and
she felt disagreeably conscious of it. Pacheco, on the
other hand, looked a model of the well-dressed gentleman. The whiteness of his shirt and vest was dazzling, a fresh carnation adorned his buttonhole, his
dog-skin gloves fitted like wax, and his whole person

betrayed marks of the most exquisite care. Two good-sized books in his hand served as the pretext for this early call.

"Here are the French novels I promised to bring you," said he in rather a loud tone, after the first greetings; for Asis made him aware by a glance that there were pirates on the coast. "If you are busy I won't intrude, but if you have ten minutes to spare may I come in?"

"With pleasure; come into the parlor. The rest of the house is not fit to be seen."

Pacheco entered the parlor. Angela closed the connecting door very quickly, but not in time to conceal the trunks, boxes and clothing scattered about.

"Are you moving, or preparing for a journey?" asked he in a dull voice, but without any tone of complaint. He did not sit down, but looked fixedly at Asis.

"Not for a journey exactly," stammered she. "I am looking over my winter clothing, putting it away in camphor, for the moths make such ravages if one is not very careful."

Pacheco came closer and lowered his voice. He spoke in the pained, melancholy tone he often used.

"You cannot deceive me. I tell you so again. I felt that you were going away before I came here this morning. You do not know me, dear. You think you can hide your thoughts from me, but you see I

divine them almost before they come into your mind.
I'm sorry you won't treat me with confidence. You
gain nothing by it in the long run, sweet hypocrite!"

Finding no suitable reply, the Marchioness lowered
her eyes and pursed up her lips in displeasure.

"Don't be angry, sweetheart. You see I am not
angry with you; only grieved. My love is her own
mistress, to go and come as she pleases. But while
you are here, why do you avoid me? Yesterday you
said we could not meet because you had an engagement for dinner!"

Moved by one impulse Asis and Diego looked
about them. The doors were shut tight, and the
muffled sound of Diabla's footsteps could be heard in
the next room. Without a word they drew closer in
order to exchange those explications which the heart
divines before the lips utter them.

"Be careful," whispered Asis, "the servants, you
know — This is unheard of for me. I never was entangled in anything of this kind before. I can't
think what possesses me. For my sake be careful!"

"Bless your little heart, dear; I know that as well
as you do. Do you think I don't know all about
you? I know that no other man has obtained the
smallest favor, not a little kiss like this one! I am
the very first. Ah! I could squeeze you to death,
my gypsy beauty!"

"Sh — Diabla — if she should hear you! Such a
girl for curiosity!"

"Just one favor.   Come to breakfast with me this morning.   Just this once!"

"You're crazy!   Sh—   Let me go!"

"Please come!   Not a soul shall know!"

"But how?   And where?"

"Out in the country.   Do come with me!   Very soon you will be rid of your torment.   Come as a farewell favor.   They allow condemned criminals a last interview!"

Why did she yield and murmur "Yes?"   Why did she give the solemn promise claimed by Pacheco?   Ah! the same old explanation.   She yielded to two motives, which since the famous sun-bath at the Saint Isidro had guided her entire conduct.   Two springs, one might say, the first of rubber — the weakness which deliberated and put off decision continually till the refuge of flight should offer protection; the other of steel, small as yet, but strong — the passion which aspired to obtain little by little complete possession and control; which was insinuating itself into her mental mechanism as the mainspring of her heart and brain.

Confiding in her promise, Pacheco presently departed; for it was highly imprudent for them to leave the house together.   Asis flew to her room to dress.   Diabla eyed her mistress with the greatest curiosity, and even ventured some feelers in regard to the interrupted packing.

"Does Madam desire me to close the trunks?

Shall Imperfecto nail down the boxes, and send to the Central for tickets?"

How should the Marchioness of Andrade reply to these ill-timed questions? Clearly with some dryness, and much inward disgust. Everything combined to exasperate her. The simplest toilet articles had disappeared in the flurry of packing. To find gloves and hat it was necessary to open several trunks. More vexations; the buckle of her pretty English walking shoes was loose, and a hook came off her waist as she was fastening it; the bottle of tooth-powder broke on the wash-basin.

"Madam will not be back for breakfast?" asked the incorrigible Diabla.

"No; I am invited to the Inzules."

"And Roque is to call for Madam?"

"Not this morning, but this evening at seven."

Diabla smiled behind her mistress's back as she stooped down to pull out the full draperies of the skirt. Asis fumed with impatience. "My fan, my gray sacque, in case it blows up cold, and my handkerchief? Where is my tulle veil? One would say those things had wings — ah! at last I am ready, heaven be praised!"

CHAPTER XVIII

SHE flew down the staircase like a bird whose prison cage has just been opened, and with the same light step hurried along the street towards the Recoletas. They had chosen for trysting place the memorable spot where Pacheco had thrown away his cigar, almost opposite the Cybele Fountain. Asis walked along under the shade of her parasol, yet bathed and animated by the sun — the sun, instigator and accomplice of that romance without preliminaries, without end and without excuse! She scanned the clumps of trees, the open gardens, the entrance to the Carrera and the distant Museum without discovering any one. Had Diego tired of waiting? Would he disappoint her so? An instant later, she heard an eager voice behind whisper,

"Over there among the trees. The hack."

Without waiting for a rejoinder, Pacheco guided her towards the rickety vehicle, one of those dirty cabs with cracked, evil-smelling gutta-percha lining, dingy windows and half-drunk driver, which ply throughout Madrid, furthering the dispatch of business and the secrecy of love. Asis entered with some scruple, thinking that her gallant might have selected a less dilapidated conveyance. Pacheco politely went round to the other door, and threw something into her lap as he entered. How charming! A bunch of roses, or rather a loosely-tied mass of rose-laden branches, still wet with dew! The whole carriage was flooded with freshness and perfume.

" These deuced coaches are so musty !" exclaimed Pacheco, as if to excuse his gallantry. But Asis darted him a glance of gratitude. Then at once the rheumatic vehicle began to rumble off. Apparently the coachman had received his orders.

" Might one venture to inquire our destination, or is that a secret ? " asked the lady.

" The Ventas del Espiritu Santo."

" The Ventas ! " exclaimed Asis in alarm. " But that is such a public place ! Do you want to risk another Saint Isidro ? "

" On Sundays it is public," returned Pacheco ; " but other days you won't see a soul there. Don't be alarmed. Do you imagine I would take you where you would find yourself in a false position ? Before asking you to come I made inquiries about all the different ways of breakfasting in Madrid. We could go to a good city restaurant or café, but we might as well advertise ourselves by the town crier ; or to some respectable, quiet confectioner's in the suburbs, but there we could not have a private room, and you might find yourself in company of bull-fighters. As for the hotels, I need not tell you the objections to them. The only other places are the Ventas and the Puente de Vallecas. Of these I believe the Ventas is the prettier."

Pretty! Asis looked out at the section they were entering. Having left behind the shade of the Retiro and the coquettish buildings of the Recoletas, the lazy carriage was traversing the most desolate and squalid district imaginable, unless we compare it to the hill of Saint Isidro. The change from the fruitful zone of the Retiro to this arid suburb of Madrid was so great that it seemed more like a theatrical transformation than a reality. Like a mastiff guarding the gates of Limbo stood the statue of Espartero, a work of art as insignificant as the original. Close by, the Moorish tower of a schoolhouse disputed the palm for bad taste. Then in the immediate foreground were masses of rubbish, and a multitude of stakes which marked off dreary house lots, and on the horizon, like a parody on some great ferocious Roman amphitheatre, loomed the Bull Ring. In that semi-desert, two steps from the heart of fashionable life, the most heterogeneous edifices had taken refuge, just as in a certain room of a house the broken-down chairs, the knife-cleaning machine and the decorations for festivals will be found huddled together. Next to the school and the Bull Ring stood a biscuit-factory, and near by a great rambling shed with the sign, " The Jolly Fellows' Lunch Counter."

In the distance everything betokened desolation.
The exciseman appeared the living image of interfer-
ence and importunity.   A little donkey laden with
rabbits and hares stood hitched before his door, while
the owner, a fellow in a hairy cap, reluctantly searched
in his belt for the money representing the tax.
Farther along a group of wild, half-clad youths were
playing at tossing the bar in a desolate yellow field.
They might have stood for the savage Gauls hovering
on the outskirts of besieged Rome.   More and more
fantastic edifices came in view.   A castle of the Middle Ages, made to all appearances of cardboard, and
surrounded by a wall over which the tall crowsfoot
flaunted its gay-flowered sprays ; an inn of dismantled
but theological aspect, since it was dedicated to the
Holy Ghost ; a wretched lunch-room which honored
itself with the ambitious device, " *Tanto monta.*"   In
the distance appeared a long reddish line of buildings,
looking redder still by the reflection of the morning
sun — the brick ovens.   Above all these motley crea-
tions of man rose that supurb creation of nature, the
Guadarrama, its peaks crowned with eternal snow.

Asis experienced a grateful surprise in noting the
total absence of private carriages.   Pacheco was right,
it would seem.   They met nothing more formidable
than a horse-breaker leading a couple of beautiful
young horses, a cart drawn by an interminable number of mules, the horse-car full of noisy passengers
of the lower classes, another hack returning with

close-drawn blinds, and an orderly, proudly astride his master's chestnut. Ah! yes, one thing more. A child's funeral. A blue and white casket jolting about in the absurd hearse, with no one to follow, journeying to the grave alone in the flood of sunshine, as the cherubs take their way through the empyrean.

During the drive our lovers spoke but little. They sat hand in hand, Asis smelling at her roses, and looking out the window from time to time, with the vague idea of diminishing thus the contrabrand nature of the expedition. In her own mind she classed it as the very last of its kind, and this thought induced melancholy. The moments savored of a sweet never to be tasted again.

When the carriage reached the bridge the coachman stopped before the picturesque cluster of cafés, inns and gardens which constitute the new section of the Ventas.

"Which place do you prefer? Shall we stop here?" asked Pacheco.

"Here; this house looks clean and cheerful," answered the Marchioness, pointing out one with an entrance staircase of bright green.

Over the door in big letters suggesting a child's printing might be read, "Family Hotel. Meals at all hours with wine. Comfort and fair dealing." This building presented a curious and original appearance. You could hardly call it the Hanging Gardens of Babylon, but it was certainly a hanging restaurant.

What an ingenious system of utilizing the land surface! Below, a series of gardens, or sickly garden
patches, victims of the arid soil of the Madrid suburb.
Above, supported on pillars, the dance-halls, dining-
rooms and chambers, all connected by an outside
railed corridor. Not to give a gloomy impression of
this hanging Cythera, let us hasten to add that it was
all white-washed, clean as a bit of fresh-washed linen
drying in the sun, and gay as a goldfinch's nest in the
fork of a tree.

A middle-aged waiter ran out in his shirt-sleeves to
greet the early customers. The wrinkled, knowing
old fellow cast an inquiring glance at the young
couple.

"Breakfast," said Pacheco, laconically.

"Where shall I lay the table?" asked the man.

Pacheco looked all round and finally turned his
glance on Asis; but she had averted her face. With
the intuition of his profession the waiter understood,
and hastened to relieve them of embarrassment.

"Follow me, sir. I will take you to our pleasant-
est breakfast-room."

And turning to the left, he preceded them up a
narrow stair shaded by a clump of horse-chestnuts
and acacias in full bloom. The stairs led to a sort of
antechamber, open to the sky, which formed part of
the corridor. Opening a little door, the man stepped
aside and said in a very smooth tone,

"In this way, Madam."

The aspect of the little room relieved Asis. It was retired, mysterious, with tiny windows protected by great wooden shutters. The walls were freshly white-washed, and the furniture covered with white cotton cases. In the centre stood the dining-table, spread with a cloth white as ermine. The most agreeable thing about all this whiteness was that the sun seemed to filter through everywhere, casting a golden reflection on furniture and walls, and neutralizing the sepulchral effect which white drapery gives when it is chilly or cloudy outdoors. The waiter left them a moment, and Pacheco took the opportunity of saying to his companion with an expressive smile,

"They have brought us straight to the dove-cot."

And raising a snowy curtain which hung at one end of the little room, he disclosed a still smaller recess, entirely occupied by a single piece of furniture, white too, whiter than an orange-blossom.

"See, here is the nest," he continued, taking Asis by the hand and drawing her nearer. "I am not surprised that so many establishments of this sort exist and thrive. They are wide-awake people here. And their trade is not for a single day in the year, as at Saint Isidro; I shouldn't wonder if some of their customers subscribe by the month. Shall we take a season ticket, dearest?"

I do not know just what tone Pacheco gave to this pleasantry, which really, under the circumstances, was not so much out of place. But the Marchioness felt the hot blood surge into her cheeks, and knew that she was within an ace of crying from sheer anguish and mortification. It seemed as if Pacheco had torn her heart out. Woman is a pendulum constantly vibrating between natural instinct and acquired shame-facedness. The most delicate-minded man can never be sure that he is not wounding her invincible modesty.

CHAPTER XIX

THE turtle-doves had not installed themselves in the dove-cot without being seen and closely examined by a group of girls who were cooking a mutton-stew in the open air just in front of the restaurant opposite. They had hired the pot and stove from the restaurant-keeper for a modest sum which included fuel. As for the mutton and the rice, the girls had brought that in their aprons. For the benefit of the curious, we may say that they were all employés of the cigar-factory.

The culinary operations were superintended by a dark old woman, quick-witted, lively and more knowing than Merlin. Two little girls, six and eight years old, were romping about the fire, teasing to be allowed to look after the stew — a task for which they believed themselves specially qualified. The sharp eyes of the whole group were fastened on the Marchioness of Andrade and her escort as they passed, and a running fire of comments, punctuated with winks and nods of the most expressive nature, followed the pair up the narrow staircase. The cigar-makers spoke with the dry, clipped accent common to the lower class in Madrid. We might compare it to what the speech of Demosthenes would have been had that orator spit out a pebble with every phrase.

"Oh! They walk along as if they were afraid! But what a beauty! She's all red and white!"

"I think she's no better than she should be!"

"You never can tell.   These ladies of quality —"

"Oh! She is some one from the circus, not a real lady. What a Frenchy look she has!"

"Nothing of the kind. Don't I know? I tell you she is a society belle. They are people of rank. Wife of a Secretary, at the very least. Do you think none of those ladies come here? Simpletons! I tell you I know one. She is married to one of the biggest men in Madrid, never stepped her foot on the sidewalk in her life, lives in a house like the Queen's palace, and she carries on just horrid. Holy Virgin, what a scandal!"

"Anyway they don't seem very loving."

"Keep quiet! They are loving enough now in their nest. You will see the windows and doors barred as if it were a prison before long. They want to keep the sun out for fear it will spoil their complexions, you know."

As if to give the lie to the acute matron's prediction, at that instant the casement of the dove-cot opened, and Asis appeared, bareheaded, and looking with interest at the restaurant across the street.

"Look at her, look at her; she likes to watch them dance!" cried the cigar-girls, in a chorus.

And really the aërial corridor across the street offered at that moment a curious terpsichorean spectacle. A street piano was thumping out a stream of melody with that exasperating regularity which makes the instrument so odious. Everything was from *Cadiz*. *Cadiz* quickstep, gypsy dance from *Cadiz*, street-girls' chorus from *Cadiz!* A score of cigarmakers, children and kitchen wenches, all in Sunday attire, with wonderfully arranged hair, jumped and skipped in time to the music, making the crazy house shake at each tap of their high heels. Asis watched the burning faces whirl by in a maze of floating ribbons, blue and pink. That animation, that dance in mid-air, without men, without holiday to serve as pretext, seemed a stage effect, a chorus from a comic opera. She wondered if the girls were not paid by the restaurant keeper for enlivening the scene.

" Sh — " whispered the group below a few minutes later. " See, she has opened the door too. They want every one to see."

"Brazen creatures!"

Meanwhile the waiter was running up and down busily.

" Let us see what you're taking them! Omelet — ham — They are opening canned partridges. Oh, my!"

"I'd rather have my mutton-stew. How good it smells!"

" Sh — " whispered the waiter, trying to impress

the chatterboxes.   "Take care.   If they should hear
you !   They're such swells !"

In his attempt to express the superior quality of
his guests the waiter made an astonishing grimace,
half buffoonery, half respect for the big fee he scented
afar off.   Suddenly the old cigar-maker assumed a
certain diplomatic gravity.

"If they are as honest as the Holy Mother, why
should we risk our souls thinking evil of them ? Very
likely they are some newly married pair, or brother
and sister, or uncle and neice.   Find out about them.
And listen a minute, waiter."

She drew the man aside and exchanged a few
words with him in a whisper.   From this brief con-
ference resulted a most skilful project, conceived and
matured in the optimistic brain of Mother Donata —
for such was the old woman's name if the chroniclers
speak true.   Upstairs the lady and her lover were
whetting their appetites on the provocative olives and
delicious sardines in their close-fitting silver tunics.
Although Pacheco had ordered the choicest wines,
Asis refused to taste even the Tio Pepe or the Amon-
tillado.   The mere sight of the bottles brought back
her marine delusions so strongly that she almost
fancied herself in the cabin of an Atlantic steamer,
undergoing the first agonies of seasickness.   As she
insisted that door and windows should remain wide
open, the breakfast brought out no more than the degree of cordiality proper to a honeymoon in its last

quarter. Pacheco had completely lost his Andalusian glibness, and exhibited a dejection which changed, when the bottle of Tio Pepe was half gone, to the humorous melancholy he so often displayed.

"Do you feel bored?" the Marchioness asked every time the waiter left them alone.

"I am drowning my sorrows, Gypsy," returned the Andalusian, draining another glass of sherry which was of better vintage than the famous Manzanillo of Saint Isidro.

The waiter had just placed the partridges on the table when a baby face appeared at the door. It was a pink, open-mouthed little face, surrounded by a fringe of jetty curls. The cunning little tot stood undecided at the door, evidently lacking the courage to come in. Asis beckoned, and the bird flew into the nest without waiting for a second invitation. Then began the customary questions and flatteries.

"What's your name, little beauty? Do you go to school? Take some raisins; eat this baby olive, and taste the wine. What a face she makes at the sherry! Down with it, little drunkard! Where is your mother, and what does your father do?"

But not a syllable in reply. The little bird opened two eyes big as saucers, hung down her head, bringing her forehead forward, as bashful children do when they are petted, nibbled at the dainties, and stood with one foot on the instep of the other. Three minutes after the first migrating sparrow had flown

into the dove-cot a second appeared. The first may
have been five years old and the second nearly eight,
but more serious than the first and equally frightened.

"Here's the sister," said Asis. "They are as like
as two peas. The little one is prettier, but look at
the other's eyes. Come in, dear. She'll tell us her
father's name, since the fairies have stolen her little
sister's tongue."

The elder sister stood nailed to the door, serious
and suspicious, like a person who fears and hesitates
before throwing himself into an enterprise bristling
with difficulties. Her great eyes, which were really
Moorish in size, fire and precocious gravity, wandered
from Asis to Diego, and then to her little sister.
She meditated, abstractedly, searching for some formula of speech which seemed to evade her. In reality
she hesitated because at heart she felt a certain savage
repugnance to asking favors, due to an indomitable
fierceness of disposition which harmonized with her
African eyes. As her hesitation became prolonged a
reinforcement arrived in the person of Mother Donata, who entered the room resolutely, feigning (very
indifferently) an explosion of rage.

"Ah! such children! You little imps! Don't you
see you are bothering the lady and gentleman?
Come out of here quicker than lightning, or —"

"They are not at all in the way," said Asis. "They
have behaved very well, only that one won't come in,
and the baby won't open her mouth."

"The rogues know how to open it to eat," said Mother Donata, and very truthfully.

Pacheco rose, and very politely offered the old woman a seat. Grave and reserved in his own circle, he was always hail-fellow-well-met with the lower classes.

"Take a chair, Madam, and drink a glass of wine to all our good healths," he said.

Did her ears deceive her? Now, Mother Donata, pluck up heart. To the attack, now that the way is clear. Settle to business at once.

From the moment the old woman entered Pacheco shook off his melancholy and regained his natural flow of words. Assuming a semi-serious air he began to address all sorts of nonsense to the old lady. With mock solemnity he requested the pleasure of a tête-à-tête promenade with the honorable matron on the roof, and other pleasantries of the same type. The sly old woman took the joke, and marked her appreciation of it with puerile laughter, showing incidentally a perfect set of teeth. But in her replies she managed to introduce one point and another of the secret project which had been seething in her brain for the last half hour. You see the fact was that she worked in the Madrid factory, did the lady know? And she had four orphans to support, children of her daughter, who died of typhoid fever, heaven rest her soul! Their father died too, of hemorrhage of the lungs; he used to vomit blood by the cupful, and in

two months the poor soul was under the sod! No
one would believe it, strong fellow as he looked!
The two eldest girls worked in the factory now, but
they earned so little! If some one would only recom-
mend — for in this world everything goes by influence
and not by merit! At this point Mother Donata's
voice took on the most pathetic inflections. "Ah!
Virgin of the Dove! God forbid that your lordship
and ladyship ever know what it is to feed, clothe and
bring up five miserable women on eight or nine hard-
earned reals a day! If her ladyship, who looks so
generous and kind, should happen to know the Prime
Minister, or the superintendent of the factory, or
any personage connected with the Administration —
so that Lolilla might be apprenticed too! It would
be a charity indeed, the greatest in the world to an
unhappy family! Just two lines and a seal."

Pacheco replied to this harangue with great tact
and suavity, pulling out his card-case, jotting down
the old woman's address, and declaring that he would
speak to the President of the Council, or to the Prin-
cess Isabella (a particular friend), to the Bishop, to
the Nuncio even. In the midst of this pleasantry
there appeared behind the pleading grandmother and
the silent grandchildren two full-grown girls.

"These are the other unhappy orphans," explained
Mother Donata.

It would be impossible to imagine anything farther removed from the classic orphan, emaciated and

black-robed, which is drawn for us by the artists of the sentimental school. They were a couple of fresh, strapping girls, heated by their dance, overflowing with gaiety and health, their cheeks and lips crimson with the roses of youth. They frisked and joked together, with much nudging of elbows to provoke laughter — a needless labor. At first sight of these nymphs Pacheco abandoned Mother Donata, and devoted himself to the new-comers. Attracted by their good looks, he became once more the honey-tongued son of Andalusia. All the sorrows which the Tio Pepe had failed to drown now took to themselves wings. With the most expressive glances, joking and lisping more than ever, Pacheco assured these princesses of the cigarette that from the instant of their entrance his one delight had been to devour them with his eyes.

"Have you just been dancing?" asked he.

"Where are your eyes?" replied the nymphs with their ready familiarity.

"Without a single man? No partners?"

"What do we care for men?"

"One likes butter on his bread! Two dry slices are as insipid as raw pumpkin, my beauties. Why didn't you call me down?"

"You? Oh! you are not at our beck and call. You don't care to look at girls like us!"

"Don't care to look at you? Do you think I've no eyes? You are as pretty as the velvet which lines the celestial vault! Come, I won't be cheated out of my dance! I insist on a round with both of you!"

Pacheco darted out like an arrow, round the airy corridor and across the bridge which connected the two restaurants, and in less than two minutes he was dancing lightly with the cigar-girls to the discords of the street piano.

CHAPTER XX

In common with her fellow Galicians, the Marchioness of Andrade possessed the faculty of locking up every strong impression in her own breast. This manner of shutting one's self up has the advantage of preventing many explosions of temper, but on the other hand the disagreeable impressions thus pigeon-holed are apt to do great damage by dry-rotting within. When Pacheco came back after a short dance, mopping his forehead and fanning himself with his hat, he found Asis apparently tranquil and good-natured, busily feeding the two little sparrows with biscuits and cheese, and listening attentively to the chatter of Mother Donata. The good lady was describing for the third time the famous bloody vomit which had caused the untimely death of her son-in-law. But the waiter, who was sharp as a steel trap, and wiser than Solomon, saw that this breakfast was not following the natural course. Accordingly, with the imposing air of a beadle ordering loafers out of a church, he intimated to Mother Donata and her brood that they must be off.

"Go along now! Haven't you bothered the lady and gentleman long enough? I never saw anything like the face of some people."

" Just hear that fellow ! " retorted Mother Donata.
" Why, the lady herself invited me to sit down.   I
am very outspoken myself, and I like any one who is
frank and kind, especially such a noble, handsome
young couple as this one, saving your presence ! "

" Any one can see that you have very delicate feelings," replied Diego, returning the compliment with
the greatest politeness.   But Mother Donata did not
retire until she had extracted a joint promise from
Asis and Diego to make the desired intercession on
Lolilla's behalf.   The little human sparrows let
themselves be kissed, and departed with their hands
full of sweets, but red-hot pincers could not have
drawn a word from them.   They did not even chirp
until they had reached the dance hall.

The waiter took the opportunity to retire also,
announcing that he would return shortly with coffee
and liqueurs.   On leaving the room he was most careful to close the door securely.   Immediately Pacheco's
eyes sought those of his companion.   She was standing up, looking about the room as if in search of
something.

" What is my treasure looking for ? " asked
Pacheco.

" For a mirror."

" Why, there is none.   Those who come here do
not care to look at their own images.   A mirror ?
Look at yourself in my eyes.   What ? You are putting on your hat, dearest ?   What is the matter ? "

"That is only to save time, for, after all, we must go as soon as we finish the coffee."

Diego drew nearer and looked Asis straight in the eyes. She avoided his examination by drawing a veil of serenity, so to speak, over her features. He took her round the waist, and drew her down on the sofa beside him, talking, laughing softly, and caressing her tenderly all the while.

"Ah! yes, yes! That is it. My darling is jealous, jealous, jealous! My queen of heaven is jealous of me!"

Asis pushed him away and drew herself up.

"You are just foolish enough to suppose," said she, "that all my thoughts are centred on you. It is your intolerable vanity which blinds you, my good friend. I am far from being jealous, and if you press me I can tell you that — "

"What can you tell me?" asked the lover, much taken aback, and losing color.

"That it is impossible to feel jealousy when one does not — "

Don Diego interrupted her with a sudden exclamation. From pale he became actually livid, and the words came out spasmodically, as if expelled by some irresistible force superior to his will.

"No need to finish — I understand, I understand! I divine your thoughts before the words rise to your lips. For the three or four hours left us to be together, the last, probably, in which we shall ever see each other, you might have been silent! You might have continued to deceive me, or at least let me deceive myself with the illusion of your affection! It speaks well for you, doesn't it, if you really came here without some fondness for me? And you thought I could believe that? You call me stupid! I may be an idler, a good-for-nothing, a prodigal, a scapegrace — call me all that, but stupid? I a fool! and in a question of petticoats above all! That is too much! But never mind. Call me what you like; only listen to this! I am going to tell you what nobody knows; what even you don't suspect, you poor child. Perhaps you have not really cared for me until to-day. But to-day, mind, you do. Say what you will, urged on by your wounded pride, to-day you love me, you adore me! Little by little I have crept into your heart, and now when you come to lose me, it will be like the end of the world! This is certain. You will see; you will see! It is your self-esteem and pride which make you take this absurd stand. You won't condescend to be jealous? Well, you are right, for that matter. In this case you have absolutely nothing to be jealous of. Nothing could be more foolish. I don't know when I shall be able to think of another woman! Cursed be the hour I saw you! No, I don't mean that. Forgive me, sweetheart! I wouldn't offend you, now or any time. I don't know what I am saying, but it is heaven's own truth that you love me!"

He poured out all this pacing the little chamber like a wild beast in a cage. Sometimes he buried his hands in his trousers pockets, sometimes he tore them out to gesticulate wildly. His countenance distorted with rage lost its indolent expression, and gained infinitely by the change. His thin features expressed character, his yellow moustache trembled, his white teeth gleamed and his azure eyes darkened like the waters of the Mediterranean when a storm threatens. The floor trembled beneath his tread. You would have thought the airy nest about to fly to pieces. That summer storm, that Southern rage was too great for the little room.

It will be remembered that the waiter had closed the door carefully when he left the dove-cot. But the window, unbarred by Asis, remained open during the whole breakfast. Our lovers took no count of this peep-hole, and considered themselves free from observation. But unfortunately the opposite dance-hall commanded a good view of their retreat, and the orphan nieces of Mother Donata were able to watch the progress of the love-tiff through the open window, while Lolilla below stirred the mutton-stew.

"Gracious! Isn't she giving it to him! And she looks mad as a hop."

"'Cause he danced with us, isn't it? I thought she wouldn't stand that!"

"Holy Virgin! He doesn't mince his words, either. What a face!"

"Look at them, look at them! He is trying everything now to bring her round. Don't put on your hat, now. Can't the silly things close the window even when they are quarrelling?"

"Who asked you to look at them?"

"What are my eyes for, silly? Sh — sh — She's as obstinate as a mule. My! Isn't she set? How she does give it to him!"

"Holy Mother, what can she have said to make him so furious? He's throwing his arms round like a windmill. What'll you bet he doesn't strike her?"

"Strike her, indeed! That's for us poor girls. Men lower the flag before these gad-about fine ladies, although any one of us could give them points on decency and virtue. Look, it seems to me that —"

"No, he is still angry."

"They will be billing and cooing in a minute — didn't I say so? Look at him — meek as a lamb — But she, no. Proud, cool, more determined than ever to put on her wrap. She wants to go. Mother of God, what those women don't know isn't worth knowing. She can wind him round her little finger. How sorry he is now. I bet you anything he goes down on his knees to try and pacify her. Look at that woman! She's like the lion in the Retiro. Determined to go. She carries her point. Look, they are starting!"

The group of cigar-girls rushed down the stairs. Asis was really going. She came down calmly, with no

appearance of haste or of displeasure ; she even smiled
at Lolilla, who was animating the fire with the bellows.
She serenely explained to the astonished waiter that
they were late already, and could not wait a minute
longer, then sent him for the coachman, who was
probably waiting for them somewhere in the shade.
Pacheco appeared crestfallen. With trembling hand
he fumbled in his pocket-book for a bill. Asis meanwhile carefully traced lines with her parasol in the
sand until she had drawn a fair design for a trellis.
When the operation was completed she stretched
out her hand mechanically and plucked a flowery
spray of acacia, which she fastened to her breast.
Mother Donata approached obsequiously, and offered
to have her grandchildren gather the lady a bunch of
acacias and poppies. Asis refused with thanks, alleging their hurry ; they must start at once. But she
went close to the old woman, and slipped something
into her hand, hard and rough as a salt herring.
Then the hack drove up. The coachman had taken
at least a couple of drinks, for his nose positively
flamed and shone in the sun like a red pepper. The
Marchioness descended the steps leading to the
bridge, Pacheco following.

"They will make up in the carriage," piped one of
the elder sparrows.

"What will you bet ? "

"Sure pop — when he gets in — "

Great was the astonishment of those unfeathered

bipeds, more talkative than musical, when after a
short parley at the carriage door, the Marchioness
offered her hand to Pacheco.   He saluted her as she
entered the carriage, which drove off at a snail's pace
down the dusty road.

"For gracious sake!   If she hasn't come out
ahead, and given him the mitten!"

"I bet he'll come back to us," declared the first-
born orphan, smoothing her large spit-curls stiff with
bandoline.

But he did not go back.   He didn't even look back
to nod a farewell, or give a last smile.   Queer fellow!
He followed the coach with his eyes until it passed
the line of brick ovens, and then with a dejected air
walked off in the opposite direction.

CHAPTER XXI

Good faith, which should be the historian's guide whether he treat of memorable events or of trivial circumstances, obliges us to declare that the Marchioness of Andrade from the time of her arrival home, about two in the afternoon, to nine in the evening devoted herself assiduously to the task of finally arranging her baggage. She had determined to leave town the following morning without fail. Packing is always a fatiguing task, and her moral disturbance made it still more so. She flew round like a will-o'-the-wisp, ransacking the remotest crannies of the house, flustering Diabla and upsetting the other servants. Her nerves, tense as guitar strings, urged her to this bustle, and she felt a continuous prick at her heart, a burning in her chest and a bitter taste in her mouth. After dinner (a mere formula that day for her) Angela asked permission to go and take leave of her sister, it being the last day in Madrid. Asis refused with a sudden burst of rage, but accorded the permission two minutes after. As soon as the maid was gone, the mistress, completely fagged out and in a worse humor than ever, retired to her chamber. She had P. P. C. cards to write, a multitude of them, but she felt so tired and so cross. More than all, the heart-prick was fast changing into a steady, intolerable pain — would it go away after an interval of rest on the bed ?   Try and see.

She closed her eyes, tasting more than ever the bitterness of gall in her mouth.   Why did she feel so wretched ?   She had acted well; had shown herself firm and dignified.   After all, the adventure was drawing to a close.   Its end was inevitable, imminent. What better conclusion than this ? Better finish thus, for if the last interview had been tender, and if — no, a hundred times better as it was.   She had been perfectly right.   It is one thing to be jealous, another to stand on self-respect and on propriety, which it is always well to remember.   Who would have supposed that — out there — in her very face, he could dance with —   She saw the aërial dance hall, the unhappy orphans jumping about, and all the incidents of the breakfast, and the bitterness became doubly bitter. Certainly it was she who had opened the window and the door ; but in any case Pacheco's behavior — Yes! he was a fine type.   A broomstick in skirts would turn his head !   A woman would be truly unhappy who believed his extravagant talk.   To court those cigar-girls so before his —   And his conceit ! Hadn't he tried to persuade her she was really in love with him at last ?   In love ?   Far from it, God be thanked !   Of course she would preserve a certain remembrance — the remembrance you —   There was that acacia flower in the locket with Maruya's hair.

What folly! Probably she would never again set eyes on Pacheco — And the pain gnawing at her heart, what did that mean? Was she really ill, or — it felt like a band of iron, pressing tighter and tighter. Gracious powers, what stupid thoughts!

Struggling thus with imagination and memory she passed into a curious state. Not sleep, but a sort of trance in which the perceptions of material life fused themselves with the delirium of fancy. It was not the nightmare caused by an overloaded stomach, in which we fall from high towers, or fly through infinite celestial zones with the same facility. Nor was it the dream provoked by the action of heat on the lobes of the brain, in which repulsive visions are represented without the sanction of the will. What Asis saw, asleep or half awake, might be represented as follows, although in reality it appeared much more vague, and curiously blurred.

She was in the train, Diabla opposite; the valise and bundle of wraps in the rack; her English veil pinned firmly over her straw hat; her travelling gloves on, her dust-coat covering her to the very chin. The train speeded on, puffing and snorting at times, and again crawling in lazy apathy across the eternal yellow plains, scorched by the tropical sun. Oh, ugly, arid, dusty Castile! Oh, level, monotonous plains! Oh, dark, disconsolate mass of the Escurial region, what happiness to lose sight of you! Oh, heat, burning of hell, when will you cease? The drawn

curtains cast a blue tinge over the whole scene, but
Asis felt the sun through them soak into her brain,
as water soaks into a sponge; felt the blood in her
veins turn to boiling pitch, and the extremity of every
nerve become a burning needle-point. The cinders
and dust of the Castilian plain blew in clouds and
whirlwinds, blinding and suffocating her. The most
desperate fanning availed nothing, for the whole atmosphere was dust, the fan brought nothing but dust
in its breezes, and the thirsty lungs drank in nothing
but burning dust particles. "Water, water; in God's
name, water! Angela, get the bottle out of the bas-
ket." Diabla fumbled in vain; nothing! The water
had been forgotten! Ah, no; at last — the flat
glass — Asis drank. "But this is no water! Manzanillo! Sherry! A burning liquid; one of those
poisons which take the reason prisoner! Oh, for a
river of my Galicia, to drink it down at one draught!"
And while she groaned out these complaints the immense solar furnace blazed on implacably, as if the
archangels and seraphs, changed into stokers, were
incessantly piling up more and more fuel to feed the
flame. And so they traversed the stony territory of
Avila, with its squadrons of enormous rocks; the
plains of Palencia; the rude deserts of Leon; the old
territory of Maragateria. "Ah! I am burning, dying!
Help!"

Ah! What has happened? We leave the level
country. Beloved mountains! Each tunnel is an

immersion in night, a bath in the depths of a well. Returning to the light of day, mountains, and more mountains, decked in shady chestnut trees, and oh, joy! leaping, frolicking brooks, and streams, cascades foaming down, and below the deep, wide Sil. The very rocks are humid, great drops ooze from the tunnel walls, the ground is covered with moisture. At first Asis revives like a fish cast back into its native element. Her heart dilates, her boiling blood cools, and the frightful thirst is appeased. But the brooks grow larger, the tunnels more frequent, and they look dark and threatening. Through them a strip of leaden sky is seen, lowering, and full of rain-laden clouds which open at last, and precipitate, first fine drops like a thick sleet, then rain, the eternal rain of the north-east, like glacial molten lead, which sobs as it brushes the window-panes. Asis feels that rain on her heart, filtering in, softening it, steeping it, until saturated, drowned in sorrow, her heart too begins to weep, drop by drop at first, then in great gushes, with a funereal gasp like —

Rap, rap. Two knocks on the door.

"Good heavens, who is that? Was I dreaming, dozing or what?"

The Marchioness felt her pillow. It was damp. Her eyes. They were wet. Tears! "Who is it? Who?"

"It is I, friend Asis, Gabriel Pardo. Do I disturb you? Please don't interrupt your packing. I met

Angela. She told me you were starting to-morrow without fail. I am so sorry to happen in at an inconvenient time, so now I'll be off."

" No, no, not for the world! Sit down ; I will be with you in a moment — I was just washing my hands."

And sure enough, there was the sound of water dashed around in the basin. But we are assured that it was her eyes the Marchioness bathed. She also made good use of the powder-puff, arranged her hair and the lace at her neck, and then felt she looked presentable. Pardo had taken up a paper, the *Epoca*, I believe, and was reading, without understanding a word he read, " The summer flight has begun. The Duke of Albares and the beautiful young Countesses of Amezaga take the Biarritz express to-day."

The two friends had scarcely time to exchange a few phrases of mutual excuse before the bell rang, and firm, manly steps were heard in the hall. From rosy-red the Marchioness turned snow-white. An involuntary smile began to play over her lips, and a brilliant light to shoot from her eyes. As Pacheco entered, Don Gabriel, in his astonishment, had difficulty in preventing himself from striking his forehead with his palm.

" At last ! " thought he. " This is the unknown ! And it is not a fortnight since their first meeting at the Duchess of Sahagun's ! Oh, woman, woman ! "

Pacheco seemed fated to offer the clearest proof of

what Pardo had already divined. Scarcely was he seated when he pulled out an English leather card-case with silver monogram, and handed it to Asis, saying in an explanatory tone,

"Marchioness, here is the address you asked me for — the cigar-maker's, you know. You may copy it, or keep the case by you as a reminder of the promise you made her."

Asis felt the perspiration start on her forehead. She did not know which way to look. What a pretext Pacheco had found to explain his late call! If Don Gabriel wanted more proof —

She stole a glance at the Major, who pretended to understand nothing, and tried to avoid looking at the famous card-case. There is no more uncomfortable position than a third in a would-be tête-à-tête. Don Gabriel could not help seeing the expressive glances which passed between Asis and Diego, and he felt on thorns to get away. However, it would not do to leave too suddenly. He took a good quarter of an hour to prepare an honorable retreat, alleging an important lecture at the Military Club as pretext. Clubs and scientific societies will always be beneficent organizations, in spite of their constitutions, since they lend themselves so readily to covering up all kinds of masculine escapades. They assist those who are in pursuit of their own pleasure, and those who, like Pardo, desire to avoid the sight of other men's joys.

Don Gabriel slackened his pace at the corner, and begin to think over the unexpected revelation. In similar cases a man rarely approves of the lady's choice. "How strangely women choose, to be sure! The devil must egg them on! But wait a bit, Gabriel Pardo. Remember that after all there is no woman in the case, only human nature. And human nature is thus constituted. Then, too, this disgust seems a bit like envy and rage — No, not that! I am not in a rage; all is, I see clearly while my poor friend is blind. How her face lit up when he came in! Truly I did not think her capable of taking a lover, least of all one of this sort. The poor girl will have a hard time of it with him, unless I am greatly mistaken. He is an Andalusian type which shows extremely well the degeneration of the Spanish race. God of our forefathers, what a country is Southern Spain! What a man that little Pacheco! Lazy, ignorant, sensual, incapable of working or serving his country; effeminate, quarrelsome, sceptical from very indolence and selfishness; useless in creating and bringing up a family, an idle cell in the social organization! And there are so many like him! And notwithstanding they thrive at times, and make a show of the talent and vivacity which is their birthright, they have no character, no seriousness, no integrity, no faith. They make bad fathers, disloyal husbands, idle citizens. Yet see them obtain honors, gain high positions. Thus wags the world. As for women, they run wild about such men. Putting generalities aside for the moment, how I pity Asis! She is of a different race. She needs to encounter a man of principle, of constancy. It is well that they are not to marry, for of course that is out of the question. Husbands are not carved out of that wood. As an adventure it may have its charm. What a strange accident! And people say there is no such thing as coincidence. Oh, card-case, card-case!"

Thus the Major. Was he unjust, or sagacious? Did he merely obey his itch for analyzing everything, or was he moved by disappointed anger? He replaced his glasses, and began to twist his beard. Where should he go?

"Well, to the Military Club, since it has lent me so honorable a pretext. They weren't ready to die of joy when I made off, were they?"

He quickened his pace after this pleasant reflection. The darkness excited him, and the group which fancy shows to every one who relieves two lovers of an unwelcome presence persisted in floating, vague and ironical, before his mental vision. Fortunately this kind of picture does not usually resist the anodyne effects of a lecture on "The Advantages and Disadvantages of a Seniority List in Professional Bodies."

CHAPTER XXII

WE will keep out of the little boudoir during the counterfire of explanations, — what can be more insipid to a third party ? — entering only when the couple are tasting the first honey of reconciliation, insipid also for you, reader ; but have patience.

Pacheco had now nothing to ask about Don Gabriel and his friendship, and Asis had forgotten the dance in the restaurant. Diego was murmuring at his lady's ear,

"And you believed I did not know you were going to-morrow ? No woman has ever yet fooled Diego Pacheco, silly child ! You had already decided this morning, that is clear ; and if you went to breakfast with me, it was only because you were a little sorry for me. You said to yourself, 'It is now only a question of hours ; I may as well gratify him this once. There will be time enough to set off the bomb and leave him to his fate !' You are thinking of it now, and sorrowfully enough, that we shall not see each other, that all our loving companionship, with its dangers and annoyances, is nearly over. Never see me, or speak to me ! Ah ! darling, you care more for me than you think ! You haven't taken the trouble to sound this little heart. Foolish child, you will remember these moments a thousand times when you are safe among your stupid country folks. And you leave behind you a man who loves you in return — just a little bit! Sweetheart! My treasure!"

The lovers were not embraced, nor even very near each other, for Pacheco occupied the arm-chair and Asis the divan. It was only their hands which sought each other, burning with the same fire, and having met, clasped and melted into one. They were silent awhile, and this was the most charming moment of all. By the mute dialogue of their eyes, and the electric contact of their palms, their spirits mingled in ineffable ecstasy. In the new and victorious sweetness of this interchange Asis felt a mixture of great surprise. She looked at Diego and believed that she had never seen him before. In his elegant figure, his countenance, his eyes, she discovered something sublime which did not really exist. But it was her fate to see it there at that moment, for so it happens in all revelations, in order that their origin, superior to inert matter and blind chance, may blaze triumphantly forth. In that moment Love revealed itself to Asis. Little by little, unconsciously, she drew Diego's hand nearer her heart, striving by that pressure to calm the sweet suffocation she experienced. Her eyes moistened, her breath quickened, and a mysterious thrill, an airy current fanned by the wings of the Ideal, vibrated through her whole being.

"Do not speak so sadly," she said, very low, with caressing softness.

"But I am sad, dearest, on account of you. I feel used up, almost ill. I don't know what I am doing, I am so bewildered. My soul is sick, and it is infecting my body; if this goes on I must take to bed. After you are gone, I shall certainly take to bed. How strange this all is! Good God, can a sane man come to such a pass?"

"You sit so far off! Come nearer, here beside me," murmured the Marchioness, in the tone of a mother speaking to a sick child.

"No; let me sit here. I am better off here. What strange changes Love works when he really gets hold of you! I don't even wish to come closer; your little hand satisfies me."

"I no longer please you, then?"

"No; not as the others have. Ah! you know only too well whether I idolize you! — but in spite of that — just now — I would rather be silent, and go no nearer you, dearest. Ah, but what is this? My sweetheart crying?"

Perhaps it was a tear; the lamp's reflection could not have shone so bright on her cheek. Diego breathed a sigh and rose, tearing away his hand.

"I'm going," said he in a voice which sounded hoarse and strained. but resolute.

Asis was on her feet in one bound, and had her arms round him, holding him back.

"No, Diego, no! What an idea; going already, when you have but just come. Why? Have you some engagement? No, I won't have you go!"

"Sweetheart — A stony road; use the goad! I have no courage to endure more now. My throat is so dry I am nearly suffocated. Why prolong the agony? This is the farewell night, and parting now we escape a few moments of pain. Good-bye, dearest. This is the best way, I believe!"

"No, no, do not go now. Because it is the last night, stay as long as possible! Diego, in the name of Heaven! Do you wish to drive me mad? No, I can't believe that you will leave me in this way!"

Pacheco took her by both arms, and looking her straight in the eyes, said very firmly,

"Consider what you say. If you keep me now, I shall stay the whole night. Reflect. Don't tell me afterwards that I over-persuaded you. The best for you is to let me go; but you shall decide."

Asis hesitated a moment. She could feel in her heart a rush of unchained passion surging up like an inundation which carries everything before it. Oh, saving, eternal principles, which Pardo so improperly termed "stereotypes"! Oh, restraining force of custom, so powerful in normal circumstances, why did ye not resist more successfully the sudden attack of that formidable torrent? Asis heard her own voice as if it were the echo of another's articulate one word,

"Stay!"

Their plan was absurd, and yet the means of putting it successfully in execution were at hand. By a fortunate coincidence Diabla was out of the house, and the cook also. It remained simply to hoodwink Imperfecto, the quintessence of stupidity, and the porter, who was sure to be nodding at that hour of the night. They arranged a bold scheme of exits and entrances which made the two delinquents shake with laughter. At midnight the house door was barred, and within it was the infringer on social dogma and divine law.

If the adventure had ended here, I sincerely believe, friendly reader, that it would not have been worth the trouble of narrating, or even of mentioning in these memoirs and conscience-scrutinies of humanity which we call novels. For although this case is so extravagant, and unpardonable; although it constitutes a daring infringement on what should not and cannot be violated, one may well suppose that in the fever of passion there is something inevitable and fatalistic corresponding to the warm fit in other fevers. But the culminating phase of this history appears to me worthy of note as rare and curious. It would be interesting to analyze it subtilely were it not preferable to leave the question as a suggestion which each reader may follow up according to the bias of his own imagination. I mean the cause, the beginning and the rapid development of the unlooked-for Idea which brought to a speedy and honorable close the adventure begun in so light and censurable a manner at the Saint Isidro.

To which of the two lovers did the idea first occur? To him, as the only cure, heroic but infallible, for his strange love-frenzy? To her, as the means of conciliating honor and passion; the instinct of uprightness and respect for duty which was always within her in spite of the weakness of her material will? Was it that the profoundly logical idea (expiatory in this case, perhaps) presents itself as the complement of real love as surely as noon follows daybreak, night follows twilight and death follows life?

Let each reader decide for himself, and imagine what paths the two spirits blazed when they lost sight of difficulties and felt no distrust in the future; shut their eyes to the problems of practical life, and waved aside the wise counsels of reason which trembles before the indissoluble, and all that bears the fearful inscription, "Forever!" and whispers that good rarely springs from evil. Let each reader reconstruct also the dialogue in which the Idea saw light — timid at first, then clear, impetuous and imperious, then triumphant, and welcomed by Love, who, crowned with roses and armed with his sharpest arrows, stood guard at the door, barring the way to all profane intruders.

For this reason, and also because I do not like to disturb any one, heaven forbid that I should enter the boudoir until it is lighted up by the sunshine. Asis stands there fresher than the dawn, with her hair streaming over her shoulders. She opens the casement fearlessly, with pride even. Every one is welcome to look now! Diego stands beside her. They both approach the window, and lean against the casement almost embraced, as though they would remove all clandestine taste from their interview, give their love a bath of solar light, and take the whole neighborhood into their confidence. You would say that the future husband and wife were about to sing a hymn of thanksgiving to their tutelary deity the sun, and offer him their first morning prayer.

"This is the great day, sweetheart," cried Pacheco; "you are to set out on your journey."

"And shall you have good weather for yours?"

"Just like this. Wait and see."

"And you can get through with your trip to Cadiz in eight or ten days?"

"On my word! Papa's approbation and all. He is longing to have me marry and settle down. I shall tell him that after the wedding I mean to run for Vigo, with the support of my father-in-law. You shall see. I am famous for making quick work of an affair — when the thing lies near my heart, you understand."

"You will write as often as you promised?"

"Little simpleton!"

"Stupid!"

"Queen of Spain!"

"In Vigo, you know — be proper."

"Oh! yes, until the priest has —" (Here Pacheco made an expressive liturgical gesture with his right hand.) "Meanwhile I shall devote myself to your baby. And what do you think? In two days I shall have won her little heart, and maybe jilted you, to take up with the younger beauty!"

A number of jesting endearments followed which need not be recorded in this veracious history. Suddenly Diego seized the right hand of his betrothed.

"Do you remember the fortune which the gypsy told you at Saint Isidro?" Then imitating the accent of the old woman he drawled out,

"One thing I see in this little hand. Something important will happen to you very soon, and nobody suspects that it is coming. You are going on a journey, but that will prove no misfortune, but will end to everybody's satisfaction. A certain person is head over heels in love with you —"

Here Diego stopped quoting the gypsy, and added out of his own presuming head,

"And you with him!"